THE KACHINA DOLL MYSTERY

by
Carolyn Keene

Illustrated by
Paul Frame

WANDERER BOOKS
Published by Simon & Schuster, New York

Published by WANDERER BOOKS
A Simon & Schuster Division of
Gulf & Western Corporation
Simon & Schuster Building
1230 Avenue of the Americas
New York, New York 10020

Manufactured in the United States of America
10 9 8 7 6 5 4 3 2

NANCY DREW and NANCY DREW MYSTERY STORIES
are trademarks of Stratemeyer Syndicate,
registered in the United States Patent
and Trademark Office
WANDERER and colophon are trademarks of Simon & Schuster

Library of Congress Cataloging in Publication Data
Keene, Carolyn.
The Kachina doll mystery.
(Nancy Drew mystery stories; 62)
Summary: At a fitness ranch in Arizona, Nancy discovers
the reason for mysterious accidents thought
to result from a curse put on the place by Hopi Indians
[1. Mystery and detective stories.   2. Hopi
Indians—Fiction.   3. Indians of North America—
Fiction]   I. Frame, Paul, ill.   II. Title.
III. Series: Keene, Carolyn. Nancy Drew mystery
stories; 62.
PZ7.K23   Nan no. 62   [Fic]   81-11381
ISBN 0-671-42346-0   ISBN 0-671-42347-9 (pbk.)   AACR2

Contents

1

A Friend's Plea

"Nancy, you have a letter from Arizona," Hannah Gruen called. "Do you know someone out there?"

Nancy Drew, her titian hair tousled by the early spring breeze, came into the kitchen through the back door. She smiled at the housekeeper, who had cared for her since her mother's death many years ago, then took the offered envelope.

"Maybe it's an advertisement," Nancy said, studying the strange figure printed in the corner of the buff-colored envelope. However, it was a handwritten letter, not a pamphlet, that she took out of the envelope.

"Why, it's from Heather McGuire," she murmured as she unfolded it to check the signature. "Remember her, Hannah?"

"The pretty girl with red hair and freckles?" Hannah asked.

Nancy nodded. "She and her older brother moved away two years ago after their parents were killed in a plane crash. We planned to keep in touch, but I got involved in solving my mysteries and I suppose she was so busy making new friends she didn't have time to write either."

"Well, is she all right?" Hannah asked.

Nancy scanned the letter and a frown marred her usually smooth forehead. "I don't know," she admitted. "Let me read this to you."

"I'll make some hot chocolate while you do," Hannah suggested. "It's rather nippy outside. You must be half-frozen after your walk."

Nancy smiled indulgently at the housekeeper. "That sounds wonderful." She began to read the letter.

> *Dear Nancy,*
> *I know you'll be surprised to hear from me after so long, but I don't know where else to turn. I remember how wonderful you have always been at solving mysteries, and now Chuck and I have one that we can't seem to do anything about.*

Nancy paused. "Chuck is her older brother," she explained.

"The one Bess used to think was so handsome," Hannah agreed.

Nancy laughed. "That's right, she was heartbroken when they told her they were going to Arizona to live with their grandfather. I'll have to call Bess and tell her about this letter."

"Does Heather say what the mystery is?" Hannah asked.

"That's the next part." Nancy went on reading.

A few years ago, Grandfather bought an old ranch near the Superstition Mountains east of Phoenix. We decided last year to make it into a fitness-health resort, and we've been working on it ever since. We planned to open by next fall when the tourist season starts here. Now, however, I'm not sure we will ever open.

"The main attraction of the ranch is a wonderful, old building that we have modernized for our hotel. Everyone calls it the Kachina House, because the old man who built it painted a number of pictures of colorful, Indian Kachina dolls on the walls

of the central hall that are beautiful.

"We finally completed work on the inside of the building and moved in just after Christmas. That's when we learned about the Kachina's curse. Absolutely nothing has gone right since, Nancy, and even Chuck is beginning to believe that there is something haunting this house. If you can't help us, I'm afraid the Kachina Health Resort will never be more than a dream.

"We have plenty of room here, so if you and possibly George and Bess could come out for a spring vacation in the desert, you would be very welcome. Once you get here, maybe you will be able to find a way to end the curse.

Nancy put the letter down with a sigh and accepted a cup of hot chocolate from Hannah.

"She sounds desperate," Hannah observed, picking up the envelope. "Is this a Kachina?" she asked, indicating the drawing in the corner.

Nancy nodded. "If I remember correctly, they are wooden statues carved by members of the southwestern Indian tribes. The dolls represent various Indian spirits. I've seen pictures of them. They are very beautiful and can be quite valuable, too."

"This one doesn't look very friendly," Hannah commented, handing back the envelope. "What are you going to do?"

"Do you think I could turn down such a plea?" Nancy asked, her blue eyes sparkling. "This sounds like a real problem, and Heather *is* an old friend." She finished her drink and got to her feet. "I think I'd better call Dad and find out if he will agree. Then I have to talk to George and Bess and see if they'd be interested in going."

Hannah watched her go with a smile, sure that Mr. Drew would not object to the trip. It had been a long winter for all of them, and the prospect of a mystery to be solved was all the young sleuth ever needed to keep her happy.

Nancy was still on the telephone talking to her father when the doorbell rang. Hannah went to admit George Fayne and her cousin Bess Marvin, Nancy's best friends. She directed them to the study, sure that Nancy would wish to talk to them at once.

"Just the two people I wanted to see," Nancy greeted them as soon as she put down the telephone receiver. "I have something to show you—a letter

11

from Heather McGuire." She handed them the note, then waited patiently while the two girls read it.

George, a slim brunette who had long ago learned to like her masculine first name, looked up first. "You are going, aren't you?" she asked.

Nancy nodded. "I just talked to Dad and he gave his permission. Now what about you two, do you want to go?"

"Do I?" George could hardly contain herself. "I'd love it. Imagine, a vacation on an Arizona ranch."

"What about the curse?" Bess asked, anxiety detracting from her pretty features.

"What about Chuck?" George teased. "You used to think he was quite something. Isn't he worth facing the curse?"

Bess giggled, showing her dimples. "Well, I guess as long as Nancy is going to be there, it will be safe enough. And I do want to help."

"Good," Nancy said. "Now why don't you call your families, then we can make some real plans."

"It's a shame the boys are all so busy at Emerson College," George commented. "They'd probably love to go to Arizona with us, Nancy."

Nancy sighed. "And I'm sure we could use their help," she admitted, thinking of her handsome friend Ned. "But we'll just have to make it on our own, I'm afraid."

Things moved quickly once George and Bess obtained permission from their families. Plane reservations were made for early Friday morning, leaving them just one day to pack the summer clothes they would need once they reached Arizona.

Nancy called Heather that evening and, though their conversation was brief, her friend's gratitude was obvious. That proved to Nancy just how worried Heather was about the rumored curse and what it could mean to her future.

Thursday, Nancy took a little time to go to the library and study the single book it had on Kachinas. The book was filled with photographs of the strange and beautiful wooden dolls, and did give her some information.

The Kachinas had originated as a part of the religion of the Hopi Indians and several other tribes. The dolls themselves represented the spirits of all the visible things in the Indian world. There were Cloud Kachinas, various animal Kachinas, plant and bird Kachinas, and even Kachinas representing abstract ideas like death or the power of the sun.

There wasn't time to read all the details that filled

the book, but as she replaced it on the shelf, Nancy realized that none of what she'd read had even hinted at the Kachinas' being involved in any curses. Could there be some other explanation for what was happening? she asked herself.

Hannah was waiting for her when she returned to the house, and she looked concerned when she handed Nancy a letter. "This came while you were out," she explained.

"It's from Arizona," Nancy observed, not recognizing the handwriting as she opened the envelope. The single sheet of paper she took out showed a crudely drawn Kachina lying on its back, an arrow protruding from it. Pasted-on letters cut from a newspaper made the message very clear.

STAY OUT OF ARIZONA, NANCY DREW.

Hannah gasped as she took the sheet from Nancy. "You can't go, Nancy," she murmured.

Nancy took a deep breath. "But I must," she said. "Don't you see, Hannah, this just proves how desperately Heather and Chuck need my help. It's obvious that no ghost sent this."

"But you could be putting yourself in danger," Hannah protested. "And your father should be told."

Nancy looked at her watch. "He's already on his way to Canada," she reminded Hannah.

"But, Nancy . . ."

"We don't want to worry him, and I'll be very, very careful, I promise," Nancy reassured her. "Now, why don't you help me with my packing? I'm never sure exactly what I should take."

Hannah's gaze told her that she wasn't fully reassured, but she followed the young detective upstairs without further protests. Nancy's heartbeat quickened as she realized that she would soon be on her way to face whoever had sent the threatening letter!

2

The Kachina's Curse

"I can't believe it," Bess said as they walked out of the terminal building into the glow of the late afternoon sun. "It was winter when we left River Heights and now it's spring."

"You'll be able to smell the citrus orchards once we leave here," seventeen-year-old Heather told them as she led the way to where her older brother Chuck was already loading their luggage into a station wagon.

"Is something wrong, Heather?" Nancy asked the slim redhead. Though their reception had been warm, she'd quickly detected a worried glint in her friend's green eyes. "Something you haven't told us?"

Chuck turned his dark head their way, his blue

eyes grave. "It's Grandfather," he said. "He's in the hospital. We took him in last night."

"My goodness," Nancy gasped. "What happened?"

"It was the Kachina's curse," Heather answered bitterly. "I didn't really want to believe in it before, but after this, I can't deny it."

"There are no ghosts," Chuck snapped, helping George, Bess, and Nancy into the back seat of the station wagon. "It was a fire in the mountains, nothing else."

Nancy frowned, sensing how troubled her friends were. "Suppose you tell me what happened," she suggested. "Maybe we can figure things out together."

Chuck got in and started the station wagon, while Heather settled herself and half-turned toward the trio in the back seat.

"It happened after we went to bed last night," Heather began, her dappling of freckles much less obvious now that her face had been tanned by the Arizona sun. "We were sleeping, but Grandfather woke up. He said he looked out the window and saw a glow of light off toward the mountains."

"A fire, you mean," Chuck corrected. "Another signal fire, no doubt."

Heather sighed. "The moon was almost full last

night, so Grandfather didn't bother to turn on any lights. He went out in the hall, and that's when he says he saw the Kachina figure."

Chuck grunted, but seemed to concentrate on the traffic as they left the airport area and moved into the city. Heather glared at him, then went on.

"Grandfather started after whatever he saw, and in the poor light, he caught his foot on a rug and fell. We found him in the hall."

Chuck nodded. "He has a broken wrist and a badly wrenched knee. The doctor says he'll have to stay in the hospital for at least a week, till his knee is healed and they're sure there isn't any other damage from the fall."

George and Bess expressed sympathy, but Nancy said very little, though her bright eyes sparkled at this new evidence of a mystery. "Has this Kachina figure been seen before?" she asked after a moment.

"Frequently, if you believe the general gossip," Heather answered. "Not that we did. I mean, we've lived there since the end of December and neither of us has seen anything."

"What about your grandfather?" George asked.

"He didn't believe the stories either," Chuck answered.

"Is there anyone else in the house who has seen

the figure?" Nancy asked. "Anyone I could talk to, I mean?"

To her surprise, Chuck and Heather exchanged glances before Heather answered. "You might ask Ngyun. He's always roaming around the place, so he might have seen something."

"Ngyun?" Nancy asked.

"He's the nephew of Maria Tomiche. She's our housekeeper now and will be the resort dietician when we open," Chuck said. "Her husband Ward teaches at the local school. He's been tutoring Ngyun so he can enter an American school in the fall."

"The boy's just been here about two months," Heather went on. "Maria's brother, Kyle Little Feather, was in Vietnam. He met and married Su Lin, Ngyun's mother, there. He'd planned to bring her and Ngyun to Phoenix as soon as he could, but things got very bad for them when the war ended. Su Lin was able to get out with Ngyun, but Kyle was killed."

"How sad," Bess murmured.

Heather nodded. "Maria didn't hear from Su Lin, didn't even know if they'd escaped till about a year ago. She was very happy when she finally got word and she's been wanting to meet Su Lin ever since, but Su Lin has been ill and finally wrote and asked if she could send Ngyun to his father's family till she was well again."

"How old is Ngyun?" George asked.

"Twelve," Chuck answered, a note of anger in his voice.

Heather giggled. "Don't mind him," she said. "He's unhappy with Ngyun at the moment."

"We just didn't need any more problems," Chuck contributed, sounding far older than twenty. "He's the real cause of Grandfather's accident, not some mysterious Kachina figure."

"What do you mean?" Nancy asked, thinking of the threatening letter she'd received.

"Grandfather was out in the hall because he thought he saw something on the mountain, and that something was probably another of Ngyun's signal fires. That kid has burned two big cactuses and one palo verde tree."

"You don't know that for sure," Heather corrected.

"Well, do you know anyone else who'd ride around the ranch starting small fires?" Chuck asked.

Heather's face was suddenly sad. "No, of course not, but he says he didn't set them, Chuck, and Maria believes him. I mean, he didn't deny starting the first fire." She turned back to Nancy. "He's never had a chance to learn much about his father's people before, and I'm afraid a lot of his ideas come from the old movies on television. He was trying to make smoke signals when he started a fire on the ridge. He was told not to do it again, but several things have been burned since."

"What about the fire your grandfather saw?" Nancy asked, pursuing the question.

"We don't really know," Chuck admitted. "By the time we got back from the hospital, there wasn't any sign of it. I suppose it could have been a trick of the moonlight." His tone made it clear, however, that he didn't believe this explanation. "Most likely though, it just burned out. Desert fires do that, if there isn't any wind."

"Nancy, do you suppose you could handle another case while you're here?" Heather asked, taking Nancy by surprise.

"What do you have in mind?" Nancy asked immediately.

"Well, it's Ngyun. The fires and some of the other things that have happened since he came to the ranch have caused a stir among the neighboring ranchers, and I was hoping that you might be able to clear his name."

"Clear his name?" Nancy frowned. "I don't understand. If he's been doing all these things, how can I help?"

Heather turned her eyes back to the roadside, with its palm and citrus trees. "I guess what I'm asking is that you investigate what has happened," she said, now gazing at Nancy. "You see, Ngyun claims that he only lit the one signal fire, and he denies leaving gates open and all the other little things he's supposed to have done. Maria believes him and, well, we really need to know. If he isn't telling her the truth, Ward says she will simply have to send Ngyun back to his mother's people."

"I'll do my best," Nancy promised, thinking that her vacation on the ranch was already promising to be a very busy one.

"How soon will we get to the ranch?" George asked, changing the subject.

"Oh, we still have quite a drive," Chuck answered. "Kachina Resort is near the Superstition Mountains." He pointed toward the east, where rugged cliffs rose out of the desert landscape.

"The Superstitions," Bess murmured. "Isn't there supposed to be some kind of lost mine in those mountains?"

"The Lost Dutchman Mine," Chuck confirmed, smiling at her. "You'll find people in Apache Junction selling maps to it."

"What is Apache Junction?" George asked.

"That's the little town closest to the ranch," Heather answered.

"Oh." Bess's round face lost a little of its usually happy expression. "I didn't realize we were going to be so far out in the country," she said.

"Don't worry, we won't let the Kachina get you," Chuck teased.

"I wasn't afraid," Bess protested. "It just seems sort of wild out here."

"We felt that way at first, too," Heather said. "But we've come to love the area now." She opened the car window. "This is my favorite time of year, too. Smell the orange blossoms."

The heavy odor drifted in on the light, spring breeze. "Orange blossoms," Bess whispered. "How romantic."

"It really is a business," Chuck corrected. "Those groves ahead are all citrus trees. A month ago, they were still loaded with oranges and grapefruit, but most of it has been picked and sold by now. We have quite a few trees on the ranch, too, so you girls can pick your own grapefruit for breakfast if you like."

"I can hardly wait," Bess said, then blushed as George and Nancy laughed.

"I'm sure Maria will have something much more

substantial prepared for us," Heather assured her. "I told her we'd wait and have dinner at the resort."

George and Bess greeted the news enthusiastically, but Nancy's mind was already on what lay ahead. Investigating a ghostly Indian figure had seemed an interesting challenge, even after the threatening letter arrived, but now that it had actually harmed someone, the whole mystery was much more serious. And, of course, there was the boy Ngyun to be considered, too. Determining his guilt or innocence in the accidents around the area could have very grave consequences for him.

"Nancy," Heather broke into her thoughts. "I'm sorry to meet you with so much bad news. It's just that having the resort means everything to all of us, and this talk of a curse could ruin us before we even start."

"Then we'll just have to stop it, won't we?" Nancy told her, hoping she sounded more confident than she felt at the moment.

Suddenly, when they were rounding a curve, a speeding car from the opposite direction swerved from its lane and came at them head on!

3

Horse Thief

Chuck had no choice but to wrench the wheel to the right and drive off the road. The girls screamed in fright as the car teetered precariously on two wheels for an instant as they moved off the hard surface. The road at this point dropped down a stony incline for a few feet until it evened out in a field overgrown with scrubby weeds.

Finally, the station wagon stalled and came to a halt in the field. Chuck's hands were still tightly clamped around the steering wheel, and he let out a deep sigh.

"That driver must have been out of his mind, coming straight at us like that!" he complained.

Bess, who had been holding on to her cousin's

26

arm, let go and shook her head in despair. Is that how people drive around here? she wondered.

"I think that man forced us off the road deliberately," Nancy declared. "He wanted us to have an accident!"

"I agree," Heather said. "But why would anyone do such a thing?"

"Maybe it has something to do with the Kachina doll mystery," Nancy said, thinking of the threatening note she had received before leaving River Heights.

"I don't know," Chuck said. "It doesn't make sense. Did anyone get the license number?"

No one had, it all had happened too fast.

"Well, let's see if we can get this car started again," Chuck said. After a few attempts, the engine turned over, and he drove along the field to a spot almost level with the road, and eased the car back onto it. Once they were again on their way, his shaken passengers calmed down.

Though the signs of habitation grew more sparse after they left Mesa, Arizona, the desert never really became desolate, for there were homes scattered throughout the area. Nancy was fascinated by the tall saguaro cactus, with their branching arms so often lifted toward the cloudless, blue sky. Since it

27

was spring, many of them wore crowns of creamy flowers.

The road narrowed and Chuck turned off onto a gravel lane. "Homestretch," he announced. "The ranch starts as we cross the cattleguard. You can see the house just over there."

Nancy followed his pointing finger, and her gasp was echoed by Bess and George. "It looks like a castle!" she exclaimed.

Heather laughed. "That's what I said the first time I saw it."

"It's really more of a fortress," Chuck said. "Those walls are several feet thick, and most of the windows weren't put in till just the last fifty or sixty years. When it was originally built, this was still Indian country and Mr. Harris meant to be safe inside."

"It looks like a part of the mountains," George observed.

"Much of the rock used in the building did come from the Superstitions," Heather acknowledged. "We decided not to change anything about the outside. I think it's more impressive just the way it is, don't you?"

"It's fantastic," Bess breathed. "I had no idea it would be anything like this."

"What are the other buildings?" Nancy asked,

forcing her gaze away from the weathered, golden-beige walls of the huge, old house.

"The low one on the right with the corrals is the stable," Heather began. "The smaller ones on the other side are extra guest cottages. There is a pool house behind the main building, and a pool, of course. There will be tennis courts and a racquet-ball court, but we don't have them done yet." She sighed. "We haven't even finished the interiors of the cottages."

"It's quite a big undertaking," Nancy acknowledged. "Do you have much help?"

"Just Maria in the house. Ward, Maria's husband, helps when he can, and Mr. Henry has let his sons Sam and Joe work for us part-time." She smiled. "Mr. Henry is our nearest neighbor. His ranch is the Circle H over that way." She pointed away from the mountains. "He's been very helpful."

"We'll be able to have ten to fifteen guests in the house itself," Chuck explained, "and when we get through, we should have room for as many as twenty in the cottages."

"What exactly will you do here?" George asked as they rode along the drive between lacy, pale green trees that were full of tiny, yellow flowers. "I mean, this isn't a dude ranch, is it?"

Chuck shook his head. "We're calling it a health

resort. What we plan to do is offer a place for people to come who want healthy outdoor exercise and a proper diet."

"Diet?" Bess's voice wasn't exactly filled with joy. Everyone laughed and she quickly joined in.

"It's not going to be just for losing weight," Heather explained, "although Maria is a dietician and will set up menus for people who do want to shed some pounds. I've studied at a studio in Mesa so I can teach aerobic dancing and rhythm fitness classes, and, if things go well, someday we may be able to put in a golf course. To start, we'll have hiking in the Superstitions, horseback riding, of course, and swimming. We hope to have a sauna ready by fall, and there will be racquetball and tennis. When people come, we'll treat them individually, setting up whatever kind of diet and exercise program they want."

"It sounds wonderful," Nancy said. "Just different enough from the ordinary resort to attract attention, but offering what more and more people are interested in—a healthy vacation."

Heather smiled at the compliment, then her happiness faded. "Healthy if we can get rid of the curse," she amended. "We can't take in a single guest if there really is some ancient apparition stalking our halls."

Chuck snorted derisively as he followed the rough driveway along the side of the old building, which was shadowed now by the thick growth of mesquite bushes and cactus. As they rounded the end of the dun-colored building, Nancy gasped in surprise. The scene ahead was totally unexpected.

A low hedge marked the line between the arid grandeur of the cactus and the dusty desert and a lush, green lawn, flowering bushes, and citrus trees, which scented the warm air. A large pool gleamed aqua in the center of the spreading gardens. A lovely, white building rose behind it, which Nancy assumed was the pool house and home of the future sauna.

"It's lovely!" she exclaimed.

"Water in the desert," Chuck explained. "We thought the contrast would be interesting for our guests."

"Shocking is more like it," George told him.

"It's like a sudden oasis," Bess agreed.

Chuck stopped the station wagon and everyone climbed out.

"Oh, I'm so glad we brought our bathing suits," Bess said. "We can lie by the pool and go home with lovely tans."

"You give them the tour, Sis," Chuck said. "I'll take the luggage in and tell Maria we're home."

"We hope to build three more cottages over there," Heather began. "They can accommodate as many as six people each, so we'll have families. It's tentative now. I mean, we can adapt our plans as we go along. Find out what our guests like best and try to supply it."

"Nothing could be lovelier than this," Nancy told her honestly. "I mean, driving up and seeing everything so completely desert and cactus, then coming around the corner to this garden. I love both aspects and I'm sure your guests will, too."

"We'll have pool parties and cookouts and maybe overnight rides into the desert or mountains, too," Heather went on. "Grandfather knows the area very well and he's been showing Chuck and me all the old trails into the mountains."

Bess sighed. "I'd love to come back when you have a lot of handsome guests to ride with."

Heather's green eyes gleamed as she winked at Nancy. "Won't you enjoy riding with Chuck?" she asked innocently. "I thought you liked him."

Bess blushed, then dimpled as she realized that she was being teased. "You're all terrible," she told them. "None of you has an ounce of romance."

"Well, right at the moment . . ." Heather began, then stopped as a door opened in the rear of the massive, stone building.

"Heather, oh, Heather, I'm so glad you're home." An Indian woman of about thirty came out into the dying sunlight. She was neatly clad in a bright, cotton print dress, and her black hair was fastened back on her neck. She would have been pretty had her expression been less troubled.

"Maria, what is it?" Heather asked, then quickly made introductions as they met on the white stone path that led from the concrete apron of the pool to the rear door of the main building.

"It's Ngyun," Maria began. "Mr. Henry just came by to ask if by any chance Ngyun had come home with an Appaloosa filly."

"What?" Heather asked.

Maria looked uncomfortable. "It seems that one is missing from the J Bar T Ranch, and someone called Mr. Henry and told him they'd seen a boy leading the horse in this direction." She paused, then added, "A boy on a black and white pinto."

"Well, has he come home with the filly?" Heather asked.

Maria sighed. "He hasn't come home at all. You know how upset he was about your grandfather's fall last night. Well, this morning he made himself a lunch and rode out. I haven't seen him since."

"Did Mr. Henry say where he was seen?" Heather asked.

Maria shook her head.

"It's not quite dinner time yet, so suppose I show my guests to their rooms. Then maybe Chuck and I can drive around and see if we can locate him," Heather said soothingly. "But don't worry so, Maria, Cochise isn't the only pinto horse around and Ngyun isn't the only boy in the area, either."

Maria smiled, but there was no happiness in her face.

"We could help you search," Nancy offered quickly. "We don't know the area, but the more pairs of eyes looking . . ." She stopped as the sound of hoofbeats came from the front of the looming building.

In a moment, a boy on a black and white pinto trotted into view. Trailing behind, held firmly by a lead rope, was a dark bay filly, whose haunches displayed the distinctive white blanket with brown spots of an Appaloosa. The boy guided the pinto right up to the hedge before stopping him.

"Hi," he called. "Look what I find running in desert. She pretty."

"Oh, Ngyun," Maria wailed. "Why . . ."

Nancy stopped the woman with a light hand on her arm. "You found the filly in the desert?" she asked, stepping forward, then introducing herself.

Ngyun smiled at her shyly, then nodded. "I know

34

she belong someone, but I afraid she get in road if I not catch her. Bring her here safe."

Heather looked at Nancy, then nodded slightly. "Why don't you take the filly and Cochise down to the stable," she suggested to the boy. "I'll go inside and call the J Bar T and tell them you found their missing horse."

The boy, who was small for twelve, nodded and turned the pinto around easily. As he rode away, Maria shook her head. "They'll call him a horse thief, won't they?" she asked no one in particular.

Heather offered no argument as Nancy and her friends followed her and Maria toward the imposing, old house. As they stepped into the shadow of the building, Nancy shivered though the day was still warm. There was, she sensed, trouble ahead!

4

Dangerous Warning

The inside of the huge building was surprising. One door led from the rear entry to a large yet cozy-looking room filled with sofas and chairs grouped for conversation or, in one corner, around a television set. A second door, the one they entered through, led into a very modern kitchen, which was filled with delicious scents.

Bess stopped and sniffed appreciatively. "This is even better than the orange blossoms," she observed.

"Dinner will be ready in about an hour," Maria said with a grateful smile. "I was working on it when Mr. Henry arrived."

"You just go ahead with what you were doing,

36

Maria," Heather told her. "I'll talk to Mr. Henry after I call the people at the J Bar T."

Maria nodded. "Thank you, Heather," she murmured.

Nancy, Bess, and George followed Heather out of the kitchen into an airy dining room. There were several tables scattered around the big room that would accommodate four or six people each, but Nancy could see that there was space for twice as many. The walls were decorated with small, Indian rugs and blankets plus a number of paintings of western and desert scenes. Indian baskets holding dried flower arrangements decorated the side tables, giving the entire room a friendly, western atmosphere.

"I'll show you to your rooms before I take care of things for Maria," Heather began. "I'm just sorry that all this has come up right now. I was hoping we could have a nice, quiet evening, but . . ."

"You don't really think the boy took the filly, do you?" George asked.

Heather sighed. "I don't want to," she replied, "but there have been so many incidents. Everything seemed fine at first, but after he started riding so much . . ."

"He's a cute boy," Bess said. "And he certainly

speaks English well for having been here such a short time."

"His mother speaks some English and she insisted that he learn it, too. Also, he's trying hard to be like his father, though he can't remember him too well. He was barely three when Kyle was killed." Heather led them into a large hall and Nancy gasped with delight.

"Are these the Kachinas?" Bess asked breathlessly.

"Our private gallery," Heather confirmed, her tone a mixture of pride and resignation as she pointed to the beautifully decorated walls of the hall. "And home of our resident ghost, I guess."

"Now, Heather, you don't really believe all those stories, do you?" The man who stepped into the long hall of Kachinas from the other side was tall, well-muscled, and weathered.

"Mr. Henry!" Heather said. "I was just coming to talk to you." She told quickly about Ngyun's appearance with the filly and his explanation of how it had come into his care.

"I'll take the filly to the J Bar T Ranch," Mr. Henry said, "and I'll report everything to them."

Only when that was settled did Heather remember her guests. She quickly introduced Nancy, George, and Bess to the rancher.

"So you're the sleuth that Chuck and Heather are counting on to capture their ghost," Mr. Henry said, shaking Nancy's hand firmly. "I had no idea you'd be so young, Miss Drew, or so pretty."

Nancy blushed, unsure what to say.

"She'll do it, too," George said firmly. "No ghost is safe around Nancy."

"I'm certainly going to do my best to solve the mystery here," Nancy agreed. "I want to help Heather and Chuck make this resort a success."

"We all do," Mr. Henry assured her. "That's why I'm concerned about the boy. He's causing a lot of trouble in the area, and Heather, you're going to need the good will of your neighbors if you want this resort to work."

"I don't see how a few childish pranks could cause so much trouble," Nancy said, her mind on the shy smile and almond eyes of the boy who'd ridden in on the pinto. He'd seemed younger than twelve and quite defenseless.

"That filly is worth a great deal of money," Mr. Henry told her. "And there have been a number of other things. We've been lucky with the fires so far, but he could light up a barn or a house next, and that wouldn't be so easy for us to ignore."

Heather gasped and Nancy could see her paling at the man's accusing tone, but before she could say

39

anything, Chuck came into the hall. A moment later, the rancher excused himself to talk to Chuck about some ranch business.

Heather turned back to the wall paintings with a sigh. "They really are beautiful, aren't they?" she said. "Someone suggested that we might be able to get rid of the ghost by painting over them, but I couldn't do that."

"Of course not," Bess agreed. "They are real art treasures."

"Which Kachinas are they?" Nancy asked. "I mean, what do they represent?"

Heather smiled and pointed out the feather-headdressed, red, white, and yellow Cloud Kachina; the feather-winged Eagle Kachina; the white-furred Bear Kachina; and finally a blue-masked, white-bodied creature known as the Prickly Pear Cactus Kachina. "The other three we haven't identified yet," she finished. "Maria says she thinks the one on the end is a Mud-head, but the other two even she doesn't recognize."

"They certainly are exotic," Nancy observed, standing in front of one of the unidentified figures, which sported a feathery topknot and a very carefully patterned body. "Your guests are going to love them."

"I hope so," Heather said with a smile. "Especially you three, since your rooms are right along this hall." She paused, then added, "I hope you and George don't mind sharing a room, Bess. We don't have all our furniture yet."

"Just being here is wonderful," Bess and George assured Heather as she pointed to the two doors that opened just beyond the bend in the hall.

"The front of the house is devoted to the lobby area and the resort office," Heather explained, "so all the bedrooms open off this hall. Grandfather, Chuck, and I have rooms at the other end at the moment, though we hope eventually to move upstairs and convert all the rooms down here for our guests."

"What about the Tomiches?" Nancy asked. "Do they live at the resort?"

"Yes, on the second floor, as a matter of fact. Ward and Chuck have been working on the modernization up there in the evenings. They have one end fixed, but that's all."

"Where did your grandfather see the Kachina spirit?" Nancy inquired, her mind returning to the reason for her visit.

Heather frowned. "Well, he said he came out of his room and started along the hall, but he'd only taken a few steps when he saw this thing in the moonlight. He thought it was an intruder, so he went down the hall in a hurry, then he caught his foot and . . . well, he said that the figure just seemed to fade into the wall about there." She indicated the Kachina that had attracted Nancy's eye.

Nancy stared at the painting for a moment, wishing that the masked face could give her some kind of clue. But the old paint was uninformative, and, after another moment, she shrugged and allowed herself to be directed to her room.

"I suppose if we're going to unpack before dinner, we'd better get started," she murmured as she stepped through the door which bore a freshly painted number on it.

"Don't feel rushed," Heather told them all. "We're just family, so Maria can hold dinner if you want to nap or something."

"Oh, no," Bess said quickly, "don't have her do that, not the way everything smelled in the kitchen. It must be nearly ready."

Nancy laughed as she closed her door and turned her attention to her suitcases, which Chuck had placed on the bench at the foot of her double bed. She got her keys out and started to open the large one first, anxious to hang her clothes in the closet so the wrinkles would come out. However, when she tried to unlock the bag, she found that it was already unlocked.

Could she have forgotten to lock it? Nancy asked herself as she opened the case. They had been rushed, but still. . . . Frowning, she began taking things out, trying hard to remember everything she'd packed and the exact order it had been put in.

Everything seemed all right, but when she reached for her new, blue knit shirt, the wrinkle in it moved and she jerked her hand back quickly. Nothing happened, so she carefully picked up one of the clothes hangers from the bed and lightly touched the "wrinkle." It moved suddenly, and to her horror, a brownish scorpion nearly two-and-a-half inches long scuttled out of her shirt, its deadly tail moving angrily!

5

A Scary Apparition

Nancy shrieked when she saw the ugly scorpion, but managed to control her nerves enough to use one of her unpacked riding boots to kill the creature before it could find a new hiding place. Only then did she catch her breath and really look at it.

"How did you get in that suitcase?" she asked the dead scorpion. "You didn't come with me from River Heights, that's for sure."

She picked up the vicious creature, with its poisonous stinger, and disposed of it in the corner wastebasket. Nancy looked around, sighing. It was possible that her unlocked case could have come open in the luggage area of the airport, or even here, but somehow she didn't think so. She had a disturbing feeling that someone had used the scorpion in another attempt to get rid of her. Was it the driver of the car that had forced them off the road when they arrived? The person who sent her the threatening note in River Heights?

In any case, her enemy obviously knew she had been invited by Heather and Chuck before she left home, and was desperately trying to keep her from solving the mystery. But who could it be? And what was his or her motive?

Nancy sighed. "This is getting stranger every minute," she said to herself. "And certainly more dangerous!"

Chuck and Heather seemed unsurprised when she casually mentioned the scorpion as they sat in the rear parlor after dinner.

"We don't see as many of them now as we did when we first moved in," Heather said, "but they are still around. It's wise to empty your shoes before you put them on in the morning, just to be sure."

"Ugh," Bess said with a shudder. "How could you do anything but scream, Nancy? I'd be scared to death if I found one."

"Then it's a good thing that we're sharing a room," George told Bess. "While you are screaming, the scorpion would just find a new place to hide."

"I don't think you'll need to worry, Bess," Chuck

said with a smile. "We had the exterminator out last week, so that little devil probably came from outside the house."

"I'm not so sure," Nancy said, then showed them the letter she'd received the day before.

Chuck looked grave after he finished reading it. "Now I'm beginning to think that scorpion was planted," he said. "And you probably are convinced that the car accident yesterday was deliberate, too."

Nancy shrugged. "I honestly don't know what to think," she admitted.

After a few moments of silence, the talk turned to other subjects, and soon the long day's excitement began to catch up with the three girls. Nancy was glad when Heather suggested that they make it an early evening. "I've invited some of our friends over for a barbecue tomorrow night," she explained. "I thought you might enjoy having a campfire in the desert."

"That sounds like fun," George and Nancy chorused.

"Without scorpions," Chuck told Bess, and they all laughed as the pretty blonde added her voice enthusiastically to theirs.

In spite of her weariness, Nancy found sleep difficult as she watched the moonlight tracing the delicate limbs of a palo verde tree which grew just beyond the single window of her room. She'd seen no more of Ngyun Little Feather, since he and the Tomiches ate in the kitchen rather than the dining room, but she found it hard to believe that the boy was a troublemaker. However, she could see no reason for anyone to falsely accuse Ngyun of starting fires or stealing the Appaloosa filly.

The Kachina paintings troubled her, too. They were beautiful and strangely fascinating, with their alien colors and forms. They were perfect for the resort, and as she'd stood in front of them, she'd felt no sensation of haunting or menace, only a kind of sadness.

Though she wasn't aware of drifting into sleep, Nancy knew as soon as she opened her eyes that a great deal of time had passed, for the moonlight no longer played brightly through her deep window. For a moment, she just lay still, then the sound came again and she sat up. Someone was out in the hall!

She slipped her feet into her shoes, trying not to think of scorpions, then pulled on her robe as she moved to the door, opening it as quietly as she could. The hall, which stretched in both directions, was dimly lit by the moonlight that came in the windows at each end, but shadows lay heavy along the inner walls and in the doorways that opened off it.

Suddenly, something moved out of the shadows at the near end of the hall and seemed to be coming toward Nancy. Sure that it was an intruder, Nancy stepped back into her room, closing the door to a crack, then peeping out. Only when the apparition reached her did she realize that it was no human form.

The Kachina drifted by, moving in and out of the shadows, seeming unaware of Nancy's eyes. Fearfully, she eased her door open and stepped out into the hall, determined to follow the creature and perhaps learn if it was real or part of a nightmare. Just then, the apparition reached the turn in the hall, and Nancy had to hurry to keep it in sight.

Her feet made soft sounds on the bare floor, but she wasn't really conscious of anything except following the Kachina. Then, suddenly, someone was coming down the stairs and a switch clicked, flooding the hall with light. The Kachina whirled for a moment, then disappeared into the wall.

"Miss Drew?" Maria Tomiche came up to her. "I thought I heard someone down here. I hope I didn't frighten you."

"Call me Nancy, please," Nancy told her, forcing

a smile though her heart was still pounding with excitement from following the Kachina.

"Were you looking for something?" the Indian woman asked.

Nancy peered around, suddenly aware that there were people sleeping behind the doors along the hall. "Could we go to the kitchen and talk?" she whispered. "I don't want to wake the others."

"Of course. Would you like some tea? I mix my own herbal blend and came down to have a cup myself. I often do when I can't sleep."

"I definitely could use a cup of tea," Nancy assured her, shivering now in reaction to her spooky vision. "I think I've just seen the Kachina ghost."

Maria nodded, seeming unsurprised as she stepped through the door that led into the kitchen. She busied herself making two cups of steaming, fragrant tea, added a small plate of pecan-rich cookies, then settled herself at the kitchen table with Nancy.

"You've seen the Kachina yourself, haven't you?" Nancy asked.

Maria nodded. "Its spirit has lived here for years, but it mostly appears when the moon is full, as it was last night and is tonight."

"You're not afraid of it?"

Maria shook her head. "The Kachinas are sacred to my people, so why should I be afraid? Besides, it has done no harm here. Mr. McGuire fell because he caught his foot in one of the small rugs, that's all."

"Do you know why the Kachinas haunt this house?" Nancy asked, suddenly sure that this quiet woman could offer her some valuable clues to the mystery she'd come to unravel.

Maria sipped her tea for a moment, then sighed. "I think it has to do with the man who built this house and the way he died," she replied.

"Do you know the story?"

"I know all the stories that were told," Maria answered evasively.

"But you don't believe them?"

Maria shrugged. "Big Jake Harris built this house and painted all the Kachinas. He was a friend of the Indians and he honored our ways. There was no reason for his death to be blamed on the old tribal chiefs. They wouldn't have scared him to death."

"What do you mean?" Nancy asked, intrigued by the woman's words. "Who said that's what happened?"

Maria looked at her suspiciously, then seemed to decide that Nancy was honestly interested. "The story is that Big Jake took something valuable from the Hopi, a treasure of some sort, and hid it in this house. When they came to reclaim it, he refused to give it up, so they threatened to burn him out or maybe they attacked the house or something. Anyway, he was a frail, old man and the fear was too much for him. He was found dead in the hall near that strange middle Kachina."

Nancy nodded, realizing that Maria must mean the spot where her apparition had disappeared. "But you don't believe that's what happened, do you?" she asked.

"My great-grandfather was among the chiefs blamed for Jake Harris's death. They were driven out of the area and died in exile in Mexico. My great-grandmother mourned him for years. She always swore that he and Jake Harris were old friends, that Jake would never have taken their treasure, so there was no reason for them to have frightened him to death."

"Do you think that's why the Kachina spirit still haunts this house?"

Maria nodded. "My great-grandfather and several of the other chiefs died shamed and alone for something they didn't do."

"Why do other people say the spirit appears?" Nancy asked, wanting to get the whole story.

"They say that the chiefs put a curse on this house because Jake Harris had hidden their treasure and they couldn't find it even after he was dead," Maria explained emotionlessly.

Nancy stared at Maria in surprise. "You mean that the treasure is still here?"

6

First Clue

Maria shrugged. "That's the story most people believe."

"But you don't?"

"People used to search this house and the surrounding area. I've heard stories about it ever since I was a little girl. No one ever found any treasure." Maria got to her feet briskly. "Would you like more tea?"

Nancy drained her cup, then shook her head. "It's delicious, but I think I should be getting back to bed. Thank you for telling me about the house and the Kachina spirit. You have given me plenty to think about."

"I just hope it helps you solve the mystery here so the McGuires can go on with the resort." Maria's expression softened. "And thank you for saying that you'd try to help Ngyun. He's really a very good boy, Miss Drew—Nancy. I just can't believe he'd do anything that would get him sent away from here. He wants so much to be like his father."

"I'll do my best on both," Nancy assured her, then made her way back through the now empty and quiet hall to her own peaceful room.

After her disturbing night, Nancy slept later than was her habit. When she'd washed and dressed in jeans and a bright, plaid Western shirt, she went outside to find Bess, George, and Heather still sitting around a table in the back garden. All three were sipping some of Maria's herb tea, their breakfast dishes empty on the table before them.

"We got too hungry to wait," Bess told her. "Anyway, we wanted you to sleep late. Maria told us that you had some excitement last night, so you would be tired."

"Did she tell you what happened?" Nancy asked, feeling rather strange about confessing to what she'd seen in the shadowy hall. It had been believable in the light of the full moon, but now that the bright Arizona sun was shining and the bees were buzzing around the citrus blossoms, it seemed more like a dream.

"She just said you'd seen something in the hall

55

and had tea with her before going back to bed," George answered, her eyes full of curiosity.

"Was it the Kachina ghost?" Heather asked as Maria came out with an omelet and a large glass of fresh-squeezed orange juice for Nancy.

Nancy recounted her night's adventures carefully, starting with the sound she'd heard in the hall. "At the time, I thought it must be an intruder," she said, "but now I realize that it was more like distant voices singing or chanting."

"An Indian chant?" George asked.

"It could have been," Nancy admitted.

"I wouldn't have followed it out into the hall," Bess murmured, shivering. "That's so spooky."

"What do you think it means?" Heather asked.

Nancy repeated the two stories that Maria had told her about the haunting of Kachina House.

Heather nodded. "I've heard both theories," she admitted. "But what does it help? Either way, we still have a ghost and we can't open our doors to guests till we get rid of it." Her voice was filled with despair. "I guess we should have sold the place to Mr. Henry when he offered to buy it last fall."

"Someone wanted it?" George asked. "You didn't tell us that."

"Oh, he wasn't interested in the old house, just the land. He has cattle, and he was going to expand his herd. We'd already done quite a bit of work on the house, though, so we didn't want to give up the resort idea."

"You sound as though you might change your mind now," Nancy observed, feeling sorry for the girl.

Heather's green eyes filled with tears. "I love it here, ghost and all, but if we can't open the resort, we'll have to sell. Grandfather invested everything we have in it. But we won't be able to maintain it, unless we make money, and we'll have to sell at a loss."

"Nancy won't let that happen," George assured her. "She'll find a way to stop the ghost."

The young detective ate her delicately spiced omelet without speaking, hoping fervently that she could justify her old friend's confidence. If the ghost had been simply someone's trickery, she would have felt surer of her next move. But last night's apparition was something she'd never encountered before, and she wasn't exactly sure what to do next.

"What would you three like to do this morning?" Heather asked, recovering her composure. "Our dinner guests won't be arriving till early afternoon, when we'll ride into the Superstitions. There's a pretty trail that leads to the place where Ward and Maria will have our dinner waiting."

"I'd like to get to know Ngyun a little better," Nancy suggested, remembering her other mystery. "Maybe he could tell us more about finding the filly."

Heather sighed. "I'm afraid he's already gone," she said. "I went to invite him to join us this afternoon, but Maria said he'd left just after dawn."

Nancy frowned. "Where does he go?" she asked.

"I don't really know," Heather admitted. "He gets on that pinto and rides out into the desert. He used to talk about learning to trail animals and watching coyotes and jackrabbits, things like that. But since the fires . . ." Her voice trailed off. "I don't think he trusts us anymore."

"Could we check the places where the fires have been set?" Nancy asked, determined to do what she could to help the unhappy boy.

"Sure," Heather replied. "You can see the blackened area up there on the ridge." She indicated a rocky ledge about a mile from the stable. "That's where he set the first one. He said he was learning to make smoke signals."

"And the others?" Nancy asked.

"Well, besides the one Grandfather thought he saw, there have been three, and the only other close one is about half a mile beyond that ridge. You can't see it from here, but when you get up on the ridge, the burned saguaro is off toward the mountains."

"So those two are within walking distance," Nancy mused.

Heather nodded. "I'd take you to see all of them today, but Chuck's already off with the jeep to run errands, and the roads are too rough for the station wagon."

"After this breakfast, I need the exercise," Nancy assured their hostess, then turned to Bess and George. "Are you ready for a nice walk in the desert?"

"You're sure you wouldn't rather lie by the pool and start a suntan?" Bess asked hopefully.

George and Nancy shook their heads, laughing.

As the three girls set off past the stable and corrals, they quickly discovered that the desert was far from desolate. The spring rains had brought green to the tufts of grass that grew everywhere, and there were delicate wild flowers on the gently rising and falling slopes of the hills that rolled toward the Superstitions. Yellow, blue, red, and white blossoms danced in the light breeze, and even the cactus exhibited flowers of varying hues.

"Why, it is really beautiful," Bess commented as

she stopped to watch a large jackrabbit bounding between two fat-bodied barrel cactuses, with their crowns of pale flowers.

"Look, there's a roadrunner," Nancy called, pointing to where the big bird was racing from one clump of grass to another. He paused, lifting his black-crested head to stare at them. Then, with a jerking of his long black tail, he was on his way again, disappearing behind a strange cactus that looked as though it was composed of monkey tails topped with scarlet flowers.

"Don't they fly?" Bess asked as the bird appeared on a small ridge ahead of them, still on his feet.

"They can," Nancy replied. "They just prefer to run."

Ahead, more desert wildlife left cover as several quail took flight. Nancy stopped, and in a moment the gray and brown birds with their dainty, black head plumes returned to the ground. Almost at once, a dozen little, yellow and brown–streaked balls of fluff emerged from the grass to join their parents. They disappeared into their thicket again as the girls detoured away from them on their walk to the ridge.

Once they reached the top, Nancy saw the charred remains of the fire. There were several stubs of scrap wood and the ends of some wooden kitchen matches. Bending closer, she could see that there were more bits of wood under the sand.

"It looks like someone tried to put this out," she observed. "Maybe Ngyun kicked sand over it and thought it was out, then it smouldered back to life."

"At least he didn't just go off and leave it to burn," Bess agreed.

"It wouldn't really matter," George contributed. "There's nothing around close enough to catch fire anyway."

"What about that cactus down below?" Bess asked, pointing toward the blackened skeleton of what had been a large and handsome saguaro cactus at the bottom of the hill.

Nancy picked up the ends of the kitchen matches and dropped them into her pocket, sure that they were a clue Ngyun had left, since she'd seen a box of kitchen matches on the big range in the resort kitchen.

The ground was rougher after they left the ridge. Small stones twisted treacherously under their feet, and the long spines of a big, prickly pear cactus reached out toward them as they slipped and slid down the incline toward the burned saguaro.

Once they reached it, Nancy looked around. "This doesn't seem like a very good place to light a signal fire," she said. "No one could see it."

"Maybe that was the idea," George suggested. "After being scolded for lighting the one on the ridge, he wouldn't have wanted anyone at the resort to see this next fire."

Nancy nodded, realizing that her friend could be correct. However, as she looked around the area of the blackened cactus, she quickly saw the difference. There was no neat pile of charred wood and, though she scraped the sandy soil all around the burned area, no sign of wooden match stubs.

"What do you think?" Nancy asked after she explained what she'd been looking for.

"I'd say this was deliberately set on fire," George said, frowning, "and not as a signal fire, either."

"But why?" Bess asked. "Why would anyone set fire to a cactus?"

Nancy could only shrug her shoulders. She was silent and thoughtful as they turned away from the blackened corpse of the saguaro. There was something wrong, and it had little to do with the burned cactus. She felt a prickling of fear and looked back just in time to see the massive saguaro sway and start to fall!

7

A Bolting Mare

There was no time to warn her friends. Nancy grabbed Bess and George by their arms and threw them and herself out of the path of the falling cactus. They all three stumbled and fell sprawling on the ground as the saguaro crashed to earth where they had been standing.

"What happened?" George gasped. "How . . .?"

"I saw it falling," Nancy explained. "I guess I must have loosened the soil at the bottom while I was searching for clues." She stopped, not sure that she believed her own words.

Bess shivered. "This place really is haunted," she observed. "Let's get back to the resort."

Nancy nodded, realizing that there was nothing else to be done here. Only the promise of the afternoon ride and the evening barbecue under the stars lifted her spirits from the unfamiliar feeling of confusion that both cases had brought her so far.

When the girls returned to the ranch and reported their experience to Chuck and Heather, he apologized for having neglected to warn them about the danger of the burned cactus.

"I've been wanting to pull it down," Chuck said. "But I just forgot about it after Grandfather was hurt. I'm glad you acted so quickly, Nancy."

"No one blames you," Nancy assured him. "And I don't think it just happened to fall down all by itself, although I was digging in the ashes around it."

"You mean—?" Bess stared at her friend in shock. The thought that someone might have toppled the cactus to hurt the girls had not occurred to her earlier.

Nancy nodded. "Could be another attempt of our unknown enemy to get rid of us. Unfortunately, I have no way to prove it."

Heather's face was worried, but she tried to cheer up her friends. "Well, whatever the reason was that the cactus fell, I think you should all relax by the pool now," she said. "Save your energy for tonight."

"That sounds like a wonderful idea," Bess agreed.

When time for the barbecue ride came, Nancy, Bess, and George were delighted to discover that the other guests were four young, male friends of Chuck's and a pert brunette that Heather introduced as Diana. Chuck had the horses saddled and waiting, and as soon as they finished the introductions, everyone went to the stable to mount up for the ride.

Chuck, with Bess riding beside him, took the lead, and Nancy quickly found herself alongside a dark-haired young man called Floyd Jerrett. He proved to be a pleasant companion as he pointed out the various formations among the weathered and somewhat overwhelming rock cliffs of the ever-closer Superstition Mountains.

"Did you ever go up there to look for the Lost Dutchman Mine?" Nancy asked.

Floyd laughed. "Everyone around here does," he answered. "I've ridden or hiked over most of the mountains since I was seven or eight. That's when I used to go out weekends with my father. We have even come across gold up there."

"From the mine?" Nancy was impressed.

"Oh, no, nothing that exciting. There are some small pockets of gold or short veins of it that wash out or are uncovered by the winter rains and floods. We've found nuggets and gold dust in the washes."

"If you girls are going to be here long enough, perhaps we can go prospecting," Tim, one of the other young men, suggested, smiling shyly at George. "We might find something, you never know."

"With Nancy's talent as a detective, we could even find the Dutchman's mine," Heather suggested from the rear of the group where she was riding with Diana's brother Paul.

"I can supply the maps," Diana offered with a giggle. "I must have twenty-five and they're all different."

"And all genuine," her date, Jerry Blake, added.

"Thanks, but I think I have quite enough mysteries at the moment," Nancy said, laughing easily.

"Nancy has seen our resident ghost," Heather told everyone.

Discussion of the Kachina spirit and the various stories about the old house kept them all busy as they rode up into the rugged mountains, following narrow trails that were flanked by sheer cliffs on one side and rather frightening, rocky slides on the other. Though Nancy loved to ride and found her bright chestnut mare Dancer a pleasure to handle, she was glad when the trail finally dropped down into a small canyon rich with trees and flowers. They reined in near the small stream that was fed by a spring.

The ranch jeep was parked at the mouth of the

canyon, and the sweet scents of food already filled the air as the young people dismounted and walked over to where Maria and her strong, dark-eyed husband were working at a small campfire. Nancy looked around and was disappointed not to find Ngyun in sight, but just as she opened her mouth to inquire about the boy, a flash of black and white appeared between the trees and he rode up to them.

Maria and Ward Tomiche greeted Ngyun with what looked like relief. When he rode to where the horses were tied, Nancy joined him. Talking to the boy was difficult at first, for he was very shy, but when she asked him about his horse, his attitude changed.

"He mine," Ngyun said. "Really mine. My grandfather say I have any horse in big herd. I take Cochise. He beautiful."

"You ride very well, too," Nancy told him. "Did your grandfather teach you?"

"Some," Ngyun answered. "We not see him much now. Uncle Ward and Aunt Maria help and Chuck. They say I like real Indian."

Nancy let the boy talk on, asking him questions about where he went and what he did. There was no hesitation in his answers, she noted. If he was lying or covering up, he was far better at it than any adult she'd ever questioned. His almond eyes fairly glowed as he talked about the deer and the wild, piglike creatures called javelina that he'd seen in the washes leading from the mountains into the desert.

"When I learn to use bow and arrows good, I hunt them," he said. "Grandfather say he bring home dinner with bow and arrows."

"Don't get too close to the javelina," Ward cautioned from the fire, where he was helping Maria set out the various dishes of food. "They may look like long-haired pigs, but they have very sharp tusks and nasty dispositions. They can be dangerous."

"Dinner is ready," Heather announced before either Ngyun or Nancy could say another word.

Never had food tasted so good. There were mounds of barbecued ribs dripping with a delicious sauce. Beans, both the traditional, baked kind and the Mexican, refried variety, were offered. There were taco chips and a green mound of guacamole dip made from avocados and onions and cottage cheese. Fresh fruits and vegetables were set out in cold water, and there was plenty of icy soda to drink.

"Don't you love our fancy china?" Heather teased, passing out battered, tin pie plates and sturdy eating utensils as well as bandana-sized napkins.

"Everything is just perfect," George assured her

as she began heaping food on her plate. "The high sides on the pie plates keep the food where it is supposed to be."

Bess sampled the refried beans, which were delicately spiced with bits of hot peppers and onions. "Oh, this is heavenly," she told Maria. "But if you're going to feed your guests like this, I don't think they'll be losing any weight."

Chuck looked up with innocent eyes. "Oh, didn't Heather tell you, we have a new method of dieting. We feed you like this, but then you have to hike back to the ranch."

Mock groans were followed by loud protest, and everyone relaxed on the grass to eat, talking contentedly of past and future rides, picnics, and barbecues. Only when the plates had been scraped clean did Bess sigh and say, "I know I shouldn't ask after all that food, but is there dessert?"

There was general laughter, but when Maria nodded, everyone turned toward her. "Indian Fry Bread," she announced. "I've brought the dough out and I'll fry it here, then you put either powdered sugar or honey inside. It makes a perfect dessert."

"Fried bread?" Bess looked dubious, but when she received the first piece and dutifully poured on the honey, her expression changed. "Why, it's wonderful!" she exclaimed. "I must find out how to make it. Everyone at home will be fascinated."

Once the food was gone, Chuck and the other young men gathered more of the nearby dead wood—fallen limbs, trees, and bushes that hadn't come back to life with spring's magic. The campfire blazed as the sun suddenly slipped beneath the horizon, plunging them quickly into night.

Ward produced a guitar from the jeep and Chuck began to play while Bess looked at him dreamily. The familiar melody soon had everyone singing along. Nancy leaned her head back, staring up at the stars, thinking how lovely and peaceful everything seemed.

"Once the moon is up, we'll have to start back," Chuck told them between songs.

"Not the way we came, I hope," Bess murmured. "I'd be afraid of missing that trail in the dark."

"No, we'll take an easier route," Heather promised. "We don't want any trouble."

While they sang, Nancy noticed that Ward and Maria had packed up all the supplies, and once the jeep was loaded, they left the canyon. Ngyun vanished, too, not waiting to ride back with them through the cooling, night air.

"I'm glad you told us to tie our jackets behind our

saddles, Heather," Nancy said, pulling hers on before she mounted Dancer. "It feels good now."

"The desert can be quite cold at night," Heather agreed. "Even in the summer, it cools off once the sun goes down."

They were quiet as they rode back, following the edge of a wash that led through the rough hills. Nancy was so deep in thought, trying to decide what to do about the Kachina spirit, that she didn't notice when the mare slowed a little. Dancer dropped behind the other horses to nibble at a tuft of grass growing on the rough hillside the trail was skirting.

Suddenly, the silence of the desert night was broken by a rattling, and Dancer whinnied, nearly unseating the young sleuth. Though she'd lost a stirrup, Nancy clenched her knees to the mare's sides, trying to keep her moving forward on the trail. But the horse was too terrified. In a moment, they were slipping and sliding down the rocky slope toward the bottom of the wash.

Frightened, Nancy grabbed the saddle horn and did her best to stay still in the saddle so as not to throw the mare off-balance as she skidded toward the hard-baked earth below. Rocks and other debris fell with them, and she could hear the shouts of the others, but at the moment everything depended on the mare's surefootedness.

Dancer's plunging ended as she stumbled to her knees, nearly throwing Nancy over her head. Still the terrified mare didn't stop. She scrambled back to her feet and leaped forward, with Nancy hanging on for dear life!

8

The Rattler

The mare stumbled again in the roughness of the wash.

Nancy regained her balance and immediately tightened her hold on the reins, trying to steady the mare. She talked to the animal as calmly as she could while her own heart was still racing from the terror of their wild descent. "Steady, girl. It's all right, Dancer," she soothed, finally succeeding in stopping the trembling creature.

"Nancy, Nancy, are you all right?" Heather called.

"I'm fine," Nancy answered, getting off the horse. "But I think we should check Dancer. She went down on her knees when we hit bottom and may have injured her legs."

In a moment, Heather, Bess, George, and the others rode back along the wash, having come down a more gradual slope further along the trail. "I have a flashlight," Heather said, taking it out of her saddlebag and dismounting to join Nancy on the ground. "What happened?" she asked as they examined the mare's slim front legs.

"It was a rattlesnake," Nancy explained. "I was riding along and all of a sudden it seemed to come down the cliff after us. I tried to keep Dancer on the trail, but she was terrified, of course. It must have been right under her hooves. Do you think she could have been bitten?"

Heather ran a hand over the mare's legs, examining them a second time. "I don't see anything," she answered. "Her knees are skinned and she's probably pretty badly bruised, but she'll make it back to the ranch all right. We'll just have to go slow. If she starts to limp, you can always ride double with someone."

"You say a rattlesnake came down the cliff after you?" Chuck asked, breaking into their examination.

Nancy nodded. "I could hear it rattling as it came."

"That doesn't make sense," Chuck said. "Rattlesnakes are shy of people. Are you sure it wasn't alongside the trail?"

"You'd already ridden by," Nancy reminded him. "If it had been along the trail, it would have been disturbed and rattling long before I got there, wouldn't it?"

"Let me have the flashlight," Chuck ordered. "And somebody hold my horse. I'll go up and see if I can find the snake."

"You be careful, Chuck," Heather warned, surrendering the flashlight to her brother.

"Are you sure you're all right, Nancy?" George asked, moving to Nancy's side now that Heather had finished examining the horse. "You weren't hurt at all?"

"Just frightened half to death," Nancy assured her. "It all happened so fast."

The others gathered around making suggestions about the snake and telling tales of their own brushes with rattlers. It was several minutes before Chuck slid back down the side of the wash.

"What did you find?" Nancy asked.

"Your rattlesnake," Chuck answered, holding out his hand so that she could see the odd-looking thing that lay in his palm. It rattled slightly from the movement, and Dancer snorted and pulled back against Nancy's steady hold on her reins.

"What is it?" Bess squeaked, stepping back just as the horse had.

"It's the rattle from a big snake," Chuck explained. "Some people cut them off dead rattlers and make them into tourist souvenirs. I found it lying on the trail."

"But how . . .?" Heather began, then turned to face Nancy, her eyes wide with fright. "Did you say it came down the cliff after you?" she asked.

Nancy nodded.

"Then someone must have thrown it from up there." Chuck uttered the words that had already begun to fill Nancy's mind with pictures of the possible consequences.

Heather gasped. "Nancy could have been injured!" she cried out. "If Dancer had lost her footing in that rock slide coming down, she could have been seriously hurt!"

"Well, nothing like that happened," Nancy said soothingly. "I'm fine and Dancer's all right, so I think we should just put this behind us and get back to the ranch." She did not want to mention their unknown enemy to Heather's friends, but she asked herself the same question Bess, George, and the McGuires did. Was this another deliberate attempt to get her off the Kachina Doll case?

The young people remounted and rode their horses along the wash. Once they reached the resort, Nancy, Bess, and George escorted the guests to their cars, but their good nights were subdued and everyone left rather quickly. Not knowing what else to do, the girls settled in the lobby, waiting for Chuck and Heather to come up from the stable.

"You think it was deliberate, don't you, Nancy?" George asked breaking the silence.

Nancy sighed. "Someone had to drop that rattlesnake down the cliff, and I was the only one riding by at the time."

"I agree," George said. "And it wasn't the Kachina spirit, either."

Nancy chuckled, "I'm sure it wasn't. As a matter of fact, the spirit seemed almost friendly last night. Whoever threw that rattler wasn't friendly at all."

"That's for sure," Heather agreed from the archway that led to the hall of the Kachina paintings. "We were just talking about that."

"And what did you decide?" Nancy asked as Chuck joined his sister in the doorway.

"That you'd better stop your investigation," Chuck replied.

"What?" Nancy looked from one to the other. "But I've just begun."

"That awful letter you showed us was bad

enough," Heather said. "And the accident and finding the scorpion in your suitcase and the toppled cactus. But this. . . . If it means things like this are going to happen, we can't let you go on, Nancy. When I wrote to you and asked you to come here, I had no idea that you would be in any kind of danger."

Chuck nodded. "The letter and the scorpion, maybe, were warnings. But you could have been killed tonight! That's more than a warning."

"I'll just have to be more careful in the future," Nancy replied firmly. "If someone is trying this hard to frighten me away, that must mean I'm making real progress, don't you think?"

Heather and Chuck seemed unconvinced, but after cups of thick, sweet, hot chocolate and cream prepared by Maria, they all went to their rooms without further discussion. A long, relaxing bath gave Nancy plenty of time to think, but she still hadn't a clue about the person who'd thrown the rattler down on her. She slipped between the cool sheets and pulled the bright quilt over her shoulders with a sigh.

She'd been asleep for several hours when the strange sounds woke her again. This time, she lay still and listened, identifying them as chanting, though she couldn't distinguish any words. After several minutes, she got up and padded to the door, quite sure what she'd find on the other side.

The Kachina she saw was much closer this time, and the moment she opened the door, it seemed to beckon to her, then moved on along the hall. Nancy followed without hesitation. As before, it floated along the hall till it reached the same painting. Then, with what appeared to be a signal of some sort, it disappeared into the painted wall, leaving Nancy alone in the hall.

Nancy stared at the painting for a long time, studying each individual section. It wasn't till her eyes reached the left hand that she realized something. The Kachina was holding what looked very much like a pencil or pen—something no Indian Kachina could possibly be concerned with!

Frowning, she went back to her room to get the powerful flashlight and the magnifying glass she kept there. Since Jake Harris had been a friend and admirer of the Indians and their Kachinas, she was sure that he wouldn't have put the writing instrument into the picture by mistake—which had to mean that it was a clue. But to what?

Using the flashlight and magnifying glass, she began to make an even closer inspection of the painting. She studied each individual brick, tracing it carefully, trying not to let her eye be confused by the complex design that Jake Harris had painted so long ago.

Eventually, she found what she was looking for. The pencil or pen was pointing to a brick that wasn't mortared into place like the others. Nancy slipped a fingernail into the tiny seam, trying to work the brick loose. It didn't move. She went back to her room for a metal nail file and used it to pry at the seam. The brick squealed and grated in protest as she dragged it out of the patterned design of the Kachina.

"Nancy?" George's head appeared around the door of the room she shared with Bess. "What in the world is going on?"

"I saw the Kachina again and it seemed to want me to investigate this painting, so . . ." Nancy lowered the brick to the floor. "Now we'll see what it wanted me to find!"

9

A Wonderful Discovery

Bess and George quickly joined Nancy as she directed the beam of the flashlight into the hole left by the brick she'd removed. The light reflected dully off what appeared to be an old, tin box.

"Have you found the Kachina's treasure?" Bess asked breathlessly. "Do you suppose the box could be full of gold?"

"I don't think so," Nancy said as she pulled the tin box out. "It isn't heavy enough."

"Maybe it has the treasure map in it," George suggested.

Nancy blew the dust off the box and lifted the lid with trembling fingers, then jumped nervously as another door opened down the hall and Heather emerged. "What's going on?" their hostess inquired as she approached the three girls.

"Nancy has found something," George explained. "The Kachina led her to it."

"What is it?" Heather asked, joining them in front of the painting.

"It looks like a diary or journal," Nancy answered, lifting an old, leather-bound book out of the tin box. She opened it with care.

"That's all that was in it?" Bess asked, taking the box and peering into it.

"It's Jake Harris's journal!" Nancy announced after she'd scanned the first page.

"Maybe he wrote something in it that will tell us where the treasure is hidden," Bess said hopefully.

"If there really is a treasure," Heather reminded her. "No one has ever been sure about that, you know."

"Look and see if there's a map," George urged.

Nancy leafed through the pages carefully. There were not a great many entries, and once the spidery script ended, there was nothing else. "No map," she told them. "Guess I'll have to read it and see if he's put a clue in his entries."

Bess, George and Heather peered over her shoulders at the open book. "I hope you *can* read it," Heather said. "His writing is so shaky and faded."

"I'll do my best," Nancy assured them. "Now, let's repair the painting and see if we can all get some sleep."

Heather shook her head. "To think that's been hidden there all these years. I wonder why no one else has ever found it."

"No one else is as good a detective," George stated firmly.

"I just followed the Kachina's guidance," Nancy told them. "It gave me the clue."

"And you investigated it and found the journal," Heather finished.

Chuck, awakened by their voices in the hall, came out to join them. He inspected the journal and listened as Nancy recounted how it had been found, then helped by replacing the brick she had pried out of the wall. That done, they all returned to their rooms. Nancy took the journal with her.

Though she was tired, she opened it at once. Even with the good light from her bedside lamp, she had difficulty reading the script. Yet she was immediately intrigued.

Deer Slayer was here today. He brought me a haunch of venison to trade for some canned goods, and we talked long about Winslow and his offer for the Ka-

*chinas. Deer Slayer doesn't want to sell
them, but the year has been a bad one and
a few of his tribe are beginning to talk of
all the food Winslow's money would buy.*

*Deer Slayer and some of the other tribe
elders have asked me to speak for them in
the bargaining with Winslow and I've
agreed, though I don't think they should
sell the figures. The ones they've let me use
to copy for my wall paintings are so beautiful, it would be a tragedy to let them go.*

Nancy turned the page as that entry ended. The
next day's writing dealt with ranch matters, a missing heifer, the possibility of sending a few calves to
the reservation for Deer Slayer's people. Later,
there was another entry about Jake's meeting with
Mr. Winslow and their discussions about the Kachinas.

*The man is offering far too little for the
Indians' treasure. He would cheat them of
the very food for their children. I've ad-
vised the chiefs and elders not to even con-
sider selling the Kachinas to him. If they
must part with them, I'm sure I can con-*

84

tact a reputable trader who will at least
make it worth their while.

Nancy yawned. Her eyes were burning from the strain of deciphering the writing. The next entry was more about his painting and the fact that Winslow had seen the pictures on the wall of the hall and acted very strangely.

> *It seems that Mr. Winslow believes that the Kachinas are here. He has taken to riding out here at odd times and even asked to be allowed to spend the night. I think he hopes to become my friend to use me against the Hopi chiefs in his trading schemes.*

Nancy stopped for a moment and stared out at the shadows of the palo verde tree. Had something moved there? she asked herself. The hair on the back of her neck prickled as though someone was watching her, yet she could see nothing.

Fully awakened by the feeling, she continued her reading. Jake seemed to be growing more and more concerned about his Indian friends and about his own safety. He described the way he'd pried the brick loose and cleared the box-sized space behind it.

> *I'll paint a Kachina to guard my hiding place, and to guide my friends to this book, should something happen to me. Perhaps it is just the fancy of an old man too long alone, but I see things in the night—fearsome torches on the distant hills and shadowy figures nearer to my house. I sleep on the second floor now, with the stairs barricaded. I'll be glad when Deer Slayer comes to visit again and I can tell him what I've learned about this man Winslow. Once he tells Winslow that the Kachinas are not for sale, perhaps my ordeal will end.*

Nancy turned the page and stopped, startled to find that there was nothing written on the next page or the one after it. In fact, a quick flipping through of the remaining pages told her that there were no more entries at all. A closer inspection of the book, however, revealed the rough edges of three or four pages that had been torn from the journal.

Frowning, she closed the old book and carefully placed it in the drawer of the nightstand, then turned off the lamp. Moonlight glowed beyond her window, and she lay watching the feathery shadows of the palo verde as it stirred in the night wind.

The entries in the journal certainly seemed to prove that Maria's theory of the old man's death was the correct one. Jake Harris had been a friend of the Hopi, not an enemy, and there appeared to be no reason for them to have hounded or frightened him to death.

And what about the stories of hidden treasure? she asked herself. Could it be the Kachinas?

That seemed more likely, though Jake hadn't mentioned seeing any except the ones he'd used as models for his wall paintings. Nancy drifted off to sleep, still not sure what clues she'd gained from her late-night discovery.

Her dreams were haunted by frail, old men and floating, teasing, beckoning Kachinas. The chanting seemed to surround her, and the Kachinas circled and reached out to her in pleading ways. It was almost a relief when a great pounding on her bedroom door brought her back to reality.

"Fire!" Chuck shouted. "We've got a fire in one of the cottages!"

10

A Raging Fire

Nancy pulled on her jeans and a sweater right over her pajamas, slipped her feet into her shoes, and raced out to the hall. George and Bess emerged right behind her.

"Wh-what happened?" Bess asked in a shaky voice.

"Let's find out," Nancy replied, and the three of them quickly followed the cold draft of night air to the open rear door.

Once outside, the situation became obvious to them instantly. "It's the cottage farthest from the house!" George cried.

The little building was blazing like a torch in the darkness. Chuck and Ward were already spraying

water from the two garden hoses on the inferno, but seemed to be making no progress at all.

Nancy looked around quickly. "Did anyone call the fire department?" she shouted above the roaring of the flames.

"I did," Heather called as she and Maria came racing from the direction of the stable. They were carrying what looked like burlap feed sacks. "They'll be along as soon as they can, but in the meantime, we'd better wet these sacks and try to keep the fire from spreading."

Nancy nodded and they all helped Heather dip the feed sacks in the swimming pool. Once they were soaked, each took a couple and began chasing the sparks that were already floating away from the blaze.

The men, having given up on the cottage, were now using the hoses to wet the walls and roofs of the nearby buildings to keep the fire from spreading. This left it up to the girls and Maria to put out the small blazes that seemed to start everywhere in the grass, the hedge, even in the clumps of desert wild flowers and bushes nearby.

It was like a nightmare. While one spark was being extinguished, three more were igniting close-by areas. The smoke rolled over them and, as it reached the stable, set the horses to whinnying in terror. When the crashing of hooves became too loud, Heather left the others and went to open the stall doors, allowing the terrified animals to get out into the corrals if they wanted to.

By the time the small, rural fire truck arrived, Nancy and the others were smoke-stained and weary. They were all glad to stand back and watch as the firemen tamed and finally put out the roaring blaze. Only then did they have a chance to relax and sit down on the damp chairs near the pool.

"How did it get started, Chuck?" one of the firemen asked, and for the first time, Nancy recognized him as Floyd, the young man she'd ridden to the barbecue with earlier that evening.

Chuck shook his head. "Your guess is as good as mine," he answered. "I was sound asleep when it started. Heather woke me up."

All eyes turned toward the redhead. "I guess it was the smell of smoke that woke me," she said. "My room faces this way and when I opened my eyes, I could see the flames. It scared me half to death. I thought the whole resort was on fire."

Floyd looked around. In the pearly beginning of daylight, the charred places on the lawn and bushes were very clear. "You're just lucky that it wasn't," he said. "If you hadn't come out in time, the place could have gone."

"Anybody out here ready for sandwiches and coffee?" Maria called from the doorway. When there was a chorus of assent, she and Ngyun emerged with two big trays.

"When in the world did you do this?" Heather asked in amazement.

"As soon as the firemen arrived," Maria answered. "I knew you wouldn't need me any more and I already had Ngyun at work making sandwiches in the kitchen."

Everyone began to eat with enthusiasm, and Ngyun's shy smile soon appeared as everyone commented on his handiwork. The ham, cheese, and beef sandwiches did taste delicious and helped to lift their spirits in the cold aftermath of the battle with the fire.

Ngyun's smile faded, however, when one of the firemen frowned at the charred and smouldering building and commented, "I just don't see how it could have started accidentally, Chuck. There wasn't anyone staying in that cottage, and you weren't working on it yesterday, were you?"

Chuck shook his head. "We finished the rough work before Grandfather's accident, and I haven't had the time to do anything else since. I've been waiting for Grandfather. He makes all the final decisions about the wiring and finishing, you know."

"Are you saying that the cottage could have been deliberately set on fire?" Nancy asked, her attention caught by the idea.

"I not do it!" Ngyun protested, getting to his feet so quickly that spilled the remainder of his milk in the grass. "I not set any fires!"

For a moment, no one spoke. Maria cleared her throat, but before she could say anything, the boy was gone, fleeing not toward the house, but toward the stable. In a moment, the black and white pinto appeared, Ngyun clinging to his bare back as they raced away from the house into the desert.

"I didn't mean to make him think I was accusing him," Nancy protested quickly, getting up. "Should I ride after him?"

"You'd never catch him," Maria told her sorrowfully.

"Why should he think you were accusing him?" George asked. "You were just asking a logical question."

"Perhaps he should be questioned," Ward observed, looking uncomfortable. "There have been so many fires since that first signal fire on the ridge. I don't think that Ngyun could have anything to do with them, but . . ." He let his voice trail off, shaking his head, then continued, "Burned saguaro cactus and fenceposts are one thing, but the cottage is something else."

"No!" Maria was on her feet, her face full of pain. "It can't be Ngyun," she cried. "Honestly, Chuck, he was in his bed when you pounded on our door. There's no way he could have done it. He wouldn't, I just know that he wouldn't."

"I think we're all jumping to conclusions," Floyd said. "The fire is too hot to check now, but I'll come back late this afternoon and look around. I'll see if I can find any clues to how it happened. Maybe that will give us some answers."

His words seemed to signal the end of the brief rest period. The firemen finished their sandwiches and coffee and began to gather up their equipment and put it back on the truck.

The rest of the group, including Nancy, Bess, and George, all set about cleaning up what they could of the debris that had been left behind. By the time the truck drove away, the sun was over the horizon and the new day had begun.

Once things had been set to right, Nancy wandered slowly toward the house. "What's wrong?" Bess asked as they started down the hall to their rooms, anxious to clean up.

"I'm worried about Ngyun," Nancy admitted. "I

promised to try to clear his name and now he thinks I've accused him of setting the cottage on fire."

"Do you believe there's a possibility that he did?" George asked.

Nancy considered, then shook her head. "I don't think he's guilty of anything except being alone too much and pretending to be the kind of boy he thinks his father was."

"Poor kid," Bess murmured compassionately. "But why would someone else set fires and let him be blamed? I mean, someone has to be doing all these things."

Nancy sighed. "I wish I knew who it was," she admitted, then brightened. "Maybe we'll find a clue after the fire cools."

"If there's a clue, you'll find it," Bess told her loyally.

After they parted, Nancy showered to remove the stains of her fire fighting, then dressed in a bright blue-and-yellow print, cotton dress. Ready to start the day, she went out to see if she could help Maria or Heather.

She found Heather alone in the lobby and asked her where Chuck was, hoping that he'd gone after Ngyun. Her hope was short-lived.

"Chuck has gone into town to talk to Grandfather. He wants to tell him about the fire and about the journal you found. Then, too, he feels he should tell him about that rattler someone threw at you last night." She frowned. "Chuck and I are still worried about you getting hurt, Nancy."

"And I'm worried about Ngyun," Nancy said, changing the subject.

Heather nodded. "So am I," she admitted, "but I don't know what to do about him. There are people who can't help setting fires, you know, Nancy. Do you think Ngyun could be like that?"

"Oh, I hope not," Nancy said, not liking the idea at all.

"Did you find out anything from the journal?" Heather asked, changing the subject.

"Not about any treasure," Nancy told her. "But it does make it clear that Jake Harris and the Indians were friends, so I very much doubt that they were the ones who caused his death."

"I'm glad of that for Maria's sake," Heather said.

"Do you think she'd like to read the journal?" Nancy asked. "Jake mentions several of the Hopi chiefs and elders by name. One of them might be her great-grandfather."

"Oh, she'd love to read it," Heather assured her. "She's always been so sure that the Indians were wrongly accused. It will make her happy to see some proof of their innocence. And after what happened this morning, I'm sure she could use some cheering up."

Nancy nodded, remembering only too well her part in Ngyun's hasty exit from their early morning gathering by the pool. "She must be very worried about Ngyun," she agreed. "I'll go and get the journal."

She hurried back to her room and opened the drawer in the bedside table. Her nails scraped the wooden bottom as she reached inside, then she stared unbelievingly into the empty drawer. The journal was gone!

11

A Flying Arrow

Nancy checked with George and Bess just to make sure that neither of them had taken the journal to read, but she wasn't surprised by their denials. "I had the feeling someone was watching me last night," she told them. "But who would take Big Jake's journal?"

"Someone who thought it might lead them to the treasure?" Bess suggested.

"Well, the thief will certainly be disappointed then," Nancy said. "There's no mention of any treasure in the journal."

Since everyone was tired from fighting the fire and from Nancy's earlier excursion in the hall following the Kachina, Maria served an early lunch so they could all settle down for naps. Afterward they planned to spend the warmest part of the afternoon in the swimming pool.

Even while she splashed in the water, however, Nancy kept watching the surrounding hills, hoping for a glimpse of the boy and the pinto horse. Later, after she'd changed out of her bathing suit, she made a search of the now smokeless ruin of the cottage. But there were no clues to be found in the charred wreckage of the building.

Floyd did no better when he came by later. "There's really not much I can tell you," he said after he finished inspecting the ruined cottage. "With so much raw wood around, it would be easy to set a small fire, and once the building was fully engulfed. . . . Unless someone saw something, I guess we'll never know for sure."

"It's just that there is no way it could have been an accident," Chuck stated as he joined them. "That's what Grandfather said when I told him. No careless cigarettes left burning, no lightning, no mice in the wiring, nothing like that. It just must have been deliberately set."

Nancy thought of the missing journal and quickly told the two young men about it. "Perhaps someone saw me reading it and set the fire to get us all out of the house," she suggested. "I mean, it *is* gone, so someone must have taken it."

"I guess if the thief thought the journal would lead him to the treasure that is supposed to be hidden here, he might do something so violent," Floyd mused. "But who could it have been?"

They all looked at Nancy, but she had no answers for them.

She continued to watch for Ngyun, and when she saw the pinto in the distance, she excused herself and walked to the stable. She stopped first at Dancer's stall, petting the mare and examining her scratched and swollen legs.

When the boy brought his horse in, Nancy went over to him and leaned on the top of the stall. "Have a nice ride?" she asked.

The boy nodded, but didn't look up at her.

"Did you happen to see any strange tracks, or anyone in a car or on horseback riding away from here?" Nancy went on.

This time the almond eyes turned her way. "Why?" Ngyun asked suspiciously.

"Someone set that cottage on fire and stole a book from my room," Nancy told him. "I thought you might have seen him."

"I go to mountains," Ngyun answered after several moments of considering the question. "No one live that way."

"But you do like to follow tracks?"

The boy nodded, his shy smile returning. "Grandfather start to teach me, but I not good yet. If he here, he trail whoever do it."

"You must know a lot about the Superstition Mountains by now," Nancy said, changing the subject as they started back toward the great, stone fortress of the resort.

"They different all the time," Ngyun answered. "Sometimes people ride or hike or dig gold. I see coyotes teach cubs to hunt and . . ."

He was interrupted by a shout from the house and excused himself politely to run to his aunt. Nancy followed more slowly, certain now that Ngyun hadn't set the fire in the cottage or taken the journal. If only she could prove it, she thought wearily. The poor boy must feel terrible, having people suspect him all the time.

Chuck came to meet Nancy, his face grim. "What did he have to say for himself?" he asked.

"About what?" Nancy was surprised by her friend's tone.

"The way he spent his day."

"He said he was riding in the mountains," Nancy answered. "Why?"

"I just got a call from Mr. Henry. One of his men rode in a little while ago to tell him that their catch pen and shed were burned, probably sometime ear-

101

ly this afternoon. The men spotted the smoke, but by the time they got there, nothing was left but charred wood."

"And you think Ngyun had something to do with it?"

Chuck's attractive features softened a little. "I don't want to think that," he admitted, "but why would anyone want to burn an old shed and corral that no one is using?"

"Why would Ngyun burn it?" Nancy countered.

"He could have been angry because Mr. Henry was the one who came over and told us about the missing filly, and Ngyun thought he was accusing him of stealing her," Chuck reminded her. "Or maybe he was just playing Indians and settlers and thought no one would notice. It is in a remote area of the Circle H."

Nancy considered for a moment, then shook her head. "I'm sure he didn't burn your cottage, and I don't think we have two firebugs in the area, do you, Chuck?"

Chuck sighed. "I have a feeling it isn't going to matter what I think," he replied bitterly. "Mr. Henry's been a good friend to us and he's been very patient about open gates and straying cattle. This time he sounded really angry. I don't know how much longer we can keep Ngyun here."

"But where would he go?"

"His mother is now staying with relatives in the Los Angeles area. Living in the city would be rough on him, but if these fires keep up. . . ." He shook his head, not bothering to finish the sentence.

Nancy started to protest, then closed her lips firmly over the words. If Ngyun was to stay, it was obvious that she must clear his name and there was no time to waste.

She and George spent the next hour walking around the desert beyond the walls of the old house, but found nothing significant.

"The ground's been so marked up by the fire truck that it's impossible to see anything," George complained.

Nancy nodded. "And we have all the hoof marks from the horses yesterday going to the barbecue site. They obscure any other tracks that might have been made."

"Let's look under your bedroom window," George finally suggested. "Perhaps we can determine whether the thief came in that way."

This idea proved more productive. Though the ground was too hard to show footprints, Nancy soon discovered something when she examined the window itself.

"Look, George!" she called out. "See all those

smudges on the frame of the screen? That proves someone lifted it down, then replaced it."

"Did you leave the window open last night?" George inquired.

Nancy nodded. "The thief had no trouble getting in this way." She stepped back, then shivered, though the late-afternoon sun was warm beyond the shadow of the house. She had the eerie feeling that they were being watched. She turned slowly, scanning the ridges and washes that formed the landscape between the ranch and the nearby mountains.

George had wandered away from the window, still trying to find a telltale set of footprints. Nancy looked after her, then shifted her attention to a clump of cactus. A roadrunner darted from it to some bushes. Quail chirped sleepily from a closer stand of grass. And a shadowy figure was moving on the crest of one ridge.

There was something so threatening about the vague movement that Nancy dodged behind a sheltering palo verde without seeing clearly what had caused the motion.

The next moment there was a whistling sound, then a "thunk" made the tree's green trunk shiver. Startled, Nancy looked up to see an arrow quivering in the wood!

12

Trapped!

"Nancy, where are you?" George called suddenly from just around the corner of the house.

Nancy looked toward the ridge. "Stay where you are," she ordered, aware that the arrow had struck the tree and not her only because she'd no longer been standing in front of the green trunk. Never looking away from the ridge, and ready to dodge into the bushes at any sign of movement, Nancy made her way around the corner to where a thoroughly unhappy-looking George waited for her.

"What in the world is going on?" George demanded.

"Someone just shot this at me," Nancy told her, extending the arrow for George's inspection. "Luckily, I saw someone moving and dodged behind the tree, or—" she shuddered, unable to finish the sentence.

"Let's go inside," George said, a frown marring her attractive features. "This is just terrible! Someone's making an attempt on your life every day!"

"But why?" Nancy asked. "Why would anyone try to harm me, George? I haven't even come close to solving either of the mysteries here. I don't know why the Kachinas are haunting the house, and I haven't been able to clear Ngyun's name." The young sleuth clenched her fist in frustration. "So far all I've done is to get Dancer injured and lose Jake Harris's journal."

"You found it first," George reminded her as they walked into the cool kitchen, where Bess was sitting at the table sipping some lemonade and sampling the cookies that Maria was taking from the oven. "You must know something dangerous to someone."

"But what?" Nancy asked, putting the arrow on the table and sinking wearily into a chair. "And whom could I be a danger to?"

"What are you talking about?" Bess inquired.

"Nancy almost got shot with this arrow," George said and explained what happened.

Bess's face turned white. "Oh, Nancy!" she cried. "What are we going to do?"

Maria had been busy taking more cookies out of the oven, and had not paid attention to the girls' conversation. Now she came over to the table and stared at the arrow.

"Where did you find this?" she asked.

"Do you know whose it is?" Nancy countered, reviving as her detective instincts returned.

"It's Ngyun's," Maria answered without hesitation. "My cousin makes arrows and he does special fletching—the feathered part—for the family. See the pattern of red feathers worked into the black and gray."

Nancy nodded. "I knew the arrow was homemade," she admitted.

"Where did you find it?" Maria asked a second time. "Don't tell me he's been shooting the cactus again."

"Someone shot it at Nancy," George spoke up. "She moved out of the way just in time, so it hit a tree."

"Nancy!" Maria paled. "You don't think . . . Ngyun wouldn't . . ." The woman sank down in the empty chair, dropping the arrow as though it had burned her fingers.

"I'm positive it wasn't Ngyun," Nancy assured her, "but how would someone else get one of his arrows?"

Maria sighed. "He's lost some by shooting them into brush or cactus," she answered, looking only slightly relieved. "My cousin gave him a dozen when Ngyun's grandfather showed him how to use the bow, and I think he has eight or nine left. Would you like me to go up and see?"

Nancy shook her head. "I don't want him to think that I suspect him of shooting the arrow at me. In fact, I think it might be a good idea not to say anything about this to anyone else." She looked at Bess and George.

"But if you're in danger, Nancy, we should tell someone," Bess protested.

"I'll just have to be more careful till I find out who wants to get rid of me," Nancy replied. "Meantime, I don't want Chuck and Heather worrying any more. And I don't want them telling their grandfather. Mr. McGuire was very disturbed when he heard about the fire. Chuck says he might have to stay in the hospital several more days because of it."

"He'd be terribly upset if he knew," Maria agreed. "But if there really is someone out there who means you harm, Nancy, you must not take any more chances. I'd rather send Ngyun back to his mother and her people than have you risk your life trying to clear his name. And you know that Chuck and Heather would feel the same way about you trying to solve their mystery."

Nancy nodded. "They've already told me that," she admitted. "But don't you see, if someone wants to hurt me, there has to be a reason. I must be close to finding out the truth, and once I do, I'll be safe."

"You just be careful," Maria warned. "Very, very careful."

The next two days passed rather quietly. The girls made trips into the town of Apache Junction, shopping in quaint, little stores for the lovely Indian jewelry that seemed to be everywhere. With Heather's expert advice, they bought beautiful, silver and turquoise belt buckles to take back to the boys, and selected more jewelry as gifts for the members of their families.

Nancy found an exquisite Kachina doll in one of the shops and was unable to resist it. "It looks just like the one painted at the far end of the hall," she told George. "Won't it make a great souvenir to show everyone when we get home?"

"When is that going to be, Nancy?" Bess asked softly, not wanting Heather to overhear them.

"How much longer are we going to stay?"

Nancy frowned. "I can't leave without solving the mysteries," she protested.

"But nothing is happening," Bess reminded her. "And you did find out what the Kachina in the hall wanted, didn't you?"

Nancy nodded. "But I still hear the chanting every night," she confessed. "I look out in the hall whenever it wakes me, but the Kachina isn't there. I have a feeling it wants me to do something else, but I don't know what."

Bess appeared unconvinced, when Heather came over with a handsome, fetish necklace to show them. There was no chance to go on with the conversation while they admired the tiny, hand-carved birds that were strung on the silver wire.

Still, memories of the words haunted Nancy through the afternoon, and after dinner she found it hard to concentrate on the card games that Chuck and Heather had suggested to fill the evening hours. A spring rainstorm seemed to be brewing, which added to the feeling of tension in the air.

After several games, Nancy excused herself and wandered into the hall to stare once more at the Kachina paintings. They were so lovely, yet eerie and, in the shadows of evening, almost frightening.

Did they conceal further secrets? she asked herself. Were there other little differences like the writing instrument that had guided her to the loose brick?

Thinking that it might give her a clue, Nancy went to her room to get her Kachina to compare it with the larger painting. However, when she reached her room, she hesitated, then went to the window to stare out at the distant flickerings of lightning that seemed to be licking into the Superstitions.

The scent of rain was in the air and on the breeze that stirred the white curtains. When she listened closely, she could hear the far-off rumbling of thunder. Then, suddenly, she heard something else— the sound of hoofbeats. In the dim light, she saw a black and white pinto headed toward one of the washes.

Nancy hesitated only a moment before racing through the house and down the path to the stable. If Ngyun was riding out in the night, she had to follow him! There wasn't even time to tell the others where she was going. If she waited, she would surely lose him in the stormy night.

Fumbling in the dark stable, Nancy saddled the bay gelding Pepper Pot and rode out as fast as she dared in the poor light. As they entered the wash, she slowed the horse a little and looked around, suddenly not sure where to go. Almost at once, she saw movement ahead, and once again there was a flash of black and white as the rider moved along the wash.

"Ngyun?" she called. "Ngyun, wait, please!"

Hoofbeats were her only answer, but since they seemed to be coming from directly ahead, Nancy urged the gelding to follow them. The wind was rising, spinning dust and small bits of sand off the top of the wash and driving them down on Nancy as she rode through the rough, ditchlike formation.

The thunder grew louder and the lightning flared more often, illuminating the scene like midday and making it easier for Nancy to guide Pepper Pot along the wash. It also gave her an occasional glimpse of the pinto's splashy haunches, but no clue to why his rider didn't slow when she called to him.

The rain came suddenly. There was a teeth-jarring crash of thunder and the skies seemed to break apart, spilling the water in sheets rather than drops. Pepper Pot slowed immediately, snorting and tossing his head, obviously wanting to turn back and run for the dry sanctuary of the stable.

Nancy allowed him to slow to a walk, then stood in her stirrups, peering ahead into the rush of water, seeking the pinto's familiar shape. However, there seemed to be nothing ahead. Nervously, Nancy urged Pepper Pot forward, following the narrowing wash as it led deeper and deeper into the hills.

"Just a little further, Pepper Pot," she told the bay. "We have to be close and Ngyun must be afraid in this storm."

The horse stumbled a little, slipping and sliding as the water gushed down the sides of the wash and turned the once hard-baked earth to mud. Lightning flashed and gave Nancy a glimpse of the scene ahead.

The wash seemed to end or at least narrow so abruptly that it was hard to imagine where a horse and rider could have gone. Yet Ngyun and Cochise were nowhere to be seen! Nancy drew her rein and waited for the next flash, berating herself for having been in too big a hurry to remember to bring her flashlight.

When the bolt came, the stark light showed only the steep walls at the end of the wash and the wet slopes of the hills above them. Then the rain increased again, pouring so hard that she could not see ten feet ahead of her. Defeated, Nancy allowed the bay to turn, weariness and despair making her slump in the saddle.

Where could Ngyun have taken Cochise? How could the boy and the pinto simply vanish out of the deep wash? Or had they even been here? For a moment, she doubted her own senses, then her courage returned and she shook her head.

"They were here, Pepper Pot," she told the gelding. "I know we were following them. I saw the pinto several times in the lightning flashes."

The gelding snorted, then suddenly plunged ahead, almost unseating her. Nancy struggled wildly to regain her balance, then tried to rein in the horse. Pepper Pot, however, had the bit in his teeth, and, fearing that she might make him fall in the rough terrain, Nancy was forced to loosen her hold again, giving him free rein.

Almost at once, she heard a strange rumbling. When she realized that it was coming from behind her, she looked back.

A wall of water cascaded through the narrow ravine, carrying with it limbs and branches torn from bushes and trees!

13

A Stormy Night

Nancy gasped as Pepper Pot headed for the steep wall of the wash. Wildly, he scrambled up the slope, barely managing to reach the top before he stopped, his sides heaving violently.

Had the horse hesitated a moment longer, Nancy knew, they both would have been carried along in the flood!

Trembling, she leaned her cheek against the horse's hot, wet neck and hugged him. He turned back to sniff at her knee, then began picking his way slowly along the ridge above the wash. Since she had no idea which way would take them back to the resort buildings, Nancy simply left the reins loose on his neck, trusting him to take them home through the stormy night.

She rode for what seemed an age before the rain ended as abruptly as it had begun. Once the pounding drops stopped, she straightened up and looked around. The wind, chilling since she was soaked to the skin, was already herding the clouds across the sky, leaving behind them black velvet sparkling with stars.

Almost at once, Nancy saw car lights ahead. They were coming in her direction and proved to be those of the battered resort jeep. It slithered to a stop beside her.

"Nancy!" George shouted, leaping out. "Thank heavens we've found you. We've been frantic. Where have you been? What happened?"

Nancy found herself lifted down from the saddle by Chuck. Once she was steady on her feet, he knotted the reins high on Pepper Pot's neck, then turned the horse loose with a slap on the haunch. "Go home, old boy," he said to him. "We'll be there to put you into your stall."

The gelding trotted off as Nancy began telling everyone exactly what had happened. "I don't know where Ngyun and Cochise could have gone," she finished. "They just weren't in the wash when I got to the end of it."

Heather frowned. "Ngyun is back at the house, Nancy," she said. "He's been there all evening. And

Cochise is in the stable. Pepper Pot was the only horse missing when we went down there looking for you."

"But I saw a rider on a pinto trotting away from the stable," Nancy protested. "And they were ahead of me in that wash. I'd never have gone so far from the house in the rain if I hadn't been following them."

"Did you really see Ngyun?" Chuck asked.

"Well, no, but . . ." Nancy stopped, then swallowed hard. "It was a trap, wasn't it?" she asked. "But how could the intruder have known that I'd follow him?"

"Maybe it didn't matter," George suggested. "I mean, maybe he just wanted you to see the pinto leaving the stable and believe that Ngyun was riding him."

Nancy nodded, her mind working feverishly. "When I followed, whoever it was must have decided it was a perfect opportunity to get rid of me. If it hadn't been for Pepper Pot, I'd have been trapped in the flood."

"You definitely picked the right horse to ride tonight," Chuck told her as he helped her into the crowded jeep. "He's saved me a couple of times."

No one said much as they bounced over the wet ground on the way back to the well-lit, stone house.

However, by the time Chuck stopped by the rear garden to let the girls out before going down to the stable to take care of Pepper Pot, Nancy had already come to a conclusion.

"Do you suppose the rider on the pinto was going to start a fire or cause some other kind of trouble?" she asked. "I mean, since I saw the horse leaving the stable, I had to believe that it was Cochise, and that would mean Ngyun could be blamed again."

"That would explain all the times someone has seen a rider on a pinto near trouble, wouldn't it?" George commented. "It's too bad you didn't get a closer look at your mystery rider."

"I will next time," Nancy promised with a sturdy smile. "Now, if you'll excuse me, I think I'll go take a nice, hot bath and get into some dry clothes."

"You come out and join us for some hot chocolate afterwards," Heather ordered gently. "I think we have some talking to do."

Nancy nodded, aware from the girl's tone that she would be asked once more to discontinue her investigation. But she couldn't stop now, the young detective realized, not when she was so close to clearing Ngyun of all the ugly accusations!

Later, however, as they sipped their hot chocolate, it took all her powers of persuasion to convince both Chuck and Heather that she had to go on with her sleuthing.

The morning dawned beautifully clear and sunny as though there'd been no storm at all. Nancy awoke, more than ready to go to work on the mystery of Ngyun's persecution. Heather offered to help by volunteering to call the nearby ranches and ask them about black-and-white pintos. By the time breakfast was over, she had a list of six possibilities to contact.

"While you do that, Heather, I think I'd like to ride out to the wash and see if I can figure out how my mysterious rider escaped," Nancy said. "Maybe I'll find a clue to his identity there."

"It seems to me we should come with you," George spoke up. "Right, Bess?"

"Just as long as we stay away from rattlesnakes and flooded washes," Bess answered.

"There's not a cloud in the sky," Nancy assured her. "I don't think we have to worry about floods."

"How about arrows and rattlers?" Bess asked.

"The only sure way to be safe is for me to find out who is pretending to be Ngyun—and why. Once we know that, we'll all be safe."

Riding along the wash in the bright sunlight was far different from the previous night, and Nancy found herself enjoying the fresh, morning air and the glimpses of all the desert creatures that seemed to be busy making their own repairs after the flood. The wash showed the marks of the racing waters, with gouges in the damp earth and the clutter of debris that had been dropped when the rain ended and the runoff slowed to a trickle.

As they rounded the bend near the end of the wash, Nancy stopped Pepper Pot and stared to her left. "I guess that's the answer to my ghostly rider's disappearance," she said, pointing to the rough trail that led from the floor of the wash to the rim. "In all the rain and confusion, I didn't even see that last night."

"Want to follow it?" George asked.

"Might as well." Nancy guided the obedient bay toward the narrow trail, then clung to the saddle as he made a rather bounding climb up it. George and Bess followed, sending a small hail of loose earth into the wash.

"It must have been someone who knows this area well," Nancy observed, looking around the open hills. "Whoever it was led me into that ravine on purpose, then got out of it just before the runoff from the surrounding hills turned it into a flood channel."

"Now we know why they call them washes," Bess murmured, looking back.

"So where do we go from here?" George asked.

Nancy considered, then pointed to a distant clump of trees. "If I'd just come out of that wash in the middle of a storm, I think I'd be looking for shelter," she said, "and those trees are the closest."

George nodded. "Heather says those spring thunderstorms never last long, so whoever it was would know that, too."

The shady ground beneath the trees was soft and still wet, since the strong Arizona sun couldn't reach it to dry it out as it had the rest of the area. Nancy dismounted at once, handing her reins to Bess. It took her only a moment to locate a set of hoofprints.

"Looks as if you were right," George said, joining her on the ground.

"It's too bad the area beyond here is so rocky," Nancy complained. "Otherwise, we could try some of Ngyun's tracking."

"The tracks lead that way," George said, following them to the edge of the trees and a few yards beyond. "Right into that loose shale."

"Now what?" Bess asked.

Nancy returned to the shade of the trees, walking under the low-hanging boughs till her eyes were

caught by a flash of bright red color on the thorny tip of a mesquite bush. She went to pick up the piece of cloth, then smiled. "Now we have two things to look for," she said triumphantly. "Someone with a pinto horse, and a red shirt or jacket with a big tear in it."

"Wonderful," George congratulated her. "Once everyone hears about this, Ngyun's name will be cleared and Maria won't have to worry about sending him to his mother."

Nancy sobered. "He'll be cleared when we *find* the person with the pinto horse and the torn clothes," she corrected, then added, "and maybe then we'll also find out why he did all these things and arranged it so they'd be blamed on Ngyun."

"It does seem strange," Bess and George agreed as the girls mounted again, and they all turned the horses toward the resort.

"Maybe Heather will have some answers for us when we get back," George suggested as they loped along.

They were feeling very pleased with their discoveries when they turned the horses loose in the corral after unsaddling them. "I hope you can get this settled so you can concentrate on the Kachina ghost," Bess told Nancy as they walked toward the rear garden.

To their surprise, no one came out to greet them, and when they entered the kitchen, neither Heather nor Maria even looked up. "Hey, Nancy found some clues," George called. "She can prove that it wasn't Ngyun in the wash last night!"

Maria turned to look at them, but there was no joy in her brown face, and Nancy could see the marks of tears on her cheeks. "What's happened?" she asked.

"It's too late," Maria sobbed, then fled from the kitchen!

14

Ngyun's Trouble

"What's happened, Heather?" Nancy asked.

"The sheriff was here," Heather replied, her own eyes filling with tears. "It was about an hour ago. He came for Ngyun. He said that some jewelry was stolen yesterday and a boy on a pinto was seen riding away from the area."

"Well, don't you listen," Nancy began. "I saw someone on a pinto last night, too, but it wasn't Ngyun, so I'm sure we can prove that the thief was the same person who tricked me into that wash."

Heather shook her head sadly. "I'm afraid no one will believe you now."

"What do you mean?" George asked. "We have a clue to the real culprit."

"It's too late," Heather sobbed.

"Why?"

"They found a stolen belt buckle in the stable. It was hidden in the saddlebags that Ngyun uses when he goes on an all-day ride and carries a lunch."

"Was that all that was taken?" Nancy asked after a moment of stunned silence. "Just a belt buckle?"

Heather stopped crying. "Well, no, but that was all they found out there. The sheriff said they would get the rest when Ngyun tells them where he's hidden it."

"How much jewelry was stolen?" Nancy continued her questioning.

"Quite a lot. The most expensive pieces were two matched squash-blossom necklaces. They were specially designed—a smaller, lighter one for the woman and a massive one for her husband. I guess they were done by a master designer, with lots of the best turquoise and the finest of silver work. There were also two or three bracelets and a couple of rings."

"Whom were they stolen from?" Nancy asked.

"From some winter visitors who have a mobile home in the desert a few miles from here. Their collection is worth a great deal of money."

"To Ngyun?" Nancy inquired gently. "What would a twelve-year-old boy want with a lot of jewelry? He's not some little thug who could pawn it."

Heather opened her mouth, but no words came out, and Nancy could see the dawning of understanding in her bright, green eyes. "That's what Maria kept saying," she murmured. "She said it had to be a mistake, that Ngyun would never take a lot of jewelry—he's not a thief."

"Perhaps we should go and talk to the sheriff, Heather," Nancy suggested. "Maybe if we explain about what happened to me last night . . ."

"We can't go anywhere till Chuck gets back with the station wagon," Heather said. "He'd already left for town before the sheriff came."

"What about the jeep?" Nancy asked.

"Ward and Maria were out with it getting supplies, so they weren't here when the sheriff came, either. Ward took the jeep and went after the sheriff and Ngyun as soon as I told him what had happened."

"Could we call the sheriff's office?" Nancy suggested.

"They weren't going there, I don't think," Heather said. "The sheriff wanted to take Ngyun to see the people who were robbed. So they could identify him and the belt buckle, I suppose."

"They'll have to say it wasn't him," Maria said from the doorway. "They'll tell the sheriff he's mistaken. It wasn't Ngyun."

"We know that, Maria," Nancy assured the woman.

Maria began to cry again. "I should have gone with Ward," she wailed. "I should be with Ngyun. He gets so frightened sometimes when he doesn't understand things. People think that just because he speaks English he understands everything, but he doesn't, and . . ."

"You were too upset," Heather reminded her. "You said yourself that you'd just frighten him more."

Maria collapsed into a chair again and Bess went to the stove to heat a kettle of water to brew the poor woman some of her own soothing tea. "What am I going to do?" Maria sobbed.

"We're going to clear him, Maria," Nancy told her firmly. "Just as soon as the sheriff comes back, I'll talk to him and perhaps we can get everything straightened out."

The words calmed Maria enough that she was soon up and bustling around making preparations for lunch. While she worked, Nancy questioned Heather about the neighbors' horses. "Several have pintos," was Heather's answer, "and no one admits to riding one last night."

Nancy sighed. "Well, I really didn't expect a confession," she admitted. "Still, it would be easier if there weren't so many."

Heather shook her head. "I just don't understand any of it," she said. "Why would anyone go to such lengths just to get a harmless boy sent away?"

"When we have the answer to that question, we'll know who is doing it," Nancy assured her.

Maria set the table with places for Chuck, Ward, and Ngyun, but when the food was ready, the men hadn't returned, so they ate without them. Though the food was excellent, no one had much of an appetite, and they were all relieved when they could busy themselves with clearing the dishes and tidying the kitchen. It helped the minutes drag by.

It was mid-afternoon before Ward drove up in the jeep. A moment later, he came in alone. Maria ran to meet him. "Where is he?" she demanded. "Where is Ngyun? Why didn't you bring him home?"

Ward's face was grim and stony, the pain showing only in his dark eyes. "The sheriff is coming with him," he replied. "He told me to go on ahead and talk to you."

"What happened?" Maria asked, the relief she'd showed before draining away. "He didn't do it, Ward, you have to believe that."

"It's not up to me to believe or disbelieve," Ward replied. "They identified him, Maria. The people said he was the one they saw riding near their trailer just before they missed their jewelry."

"But he admitted that he was in the area," Maria protested. "Heather told us that. He was on his way into the hills. Just because he rode by their mobile home doesn't mean that he did anything else."

"He had the belt buckle!"

Maria pulled away from him. "Do you believe it?" she demanded. "Do you believe that he took the jewelry?"

For a moment, Ward glared at her, then his dark eyes dropped. "I don't want to," he said, "but, Maria, what else can we believe?"

Before anything else could be said, the sheriff drove up, and in a moment Ngyun was clinging to his aunt while he tried hard not to cry.

The sheriff looked sad but stern. "Ngyun refused to tell us where the rest of the stuff is hidden," he began. "The Bascombs won't press charges if they get all their jewelry back. They had planned to leave tomorrow, so they don't want to make a big thing out of it."

"I not tell, Aunt Maria," Ngyun protested. "I not know!"

"Of course you don't, Ngyun," Maria said, hugging him for a moment. Then she held him at arm's length and said, "You must be hungry. Did you have lunch?"

The boy shook his head, and in a moment he and Maria disappeared through the archway toward the kitchen. Once they were gone, Nancy stepped forward and introduced herself to the sheriff.

With the help of George and Bess, she described her recent discoveries to him, including a full account of all that had happened to her since her arrival at the resort. She even showed him the letter she'd received before she left River Heights.

The sheriff was dubious at first, but with both George and Bess speaking up and listing some of Nancy's past accomplishments, and Heather explaining that she and her brother had invited Nancy to solve their strange case, he had to take her seriously. Maria joined them and the hope returned to her face as she listened.

"You seriously believe that someone has done all this just to frame the boy?" the sheriff asked when the young detective had finished.

Nancy nodded. "The person who rode away from the stable last night could have been there planting the belt buckle, Sheriff. Maybe my seeing him and following him was just a lucky coincidence."

"But why would anyone frame Ngyun?" The sheriff repeated his question.

Nancy swallowed a sigh. "I can't answer that question till I discover who is responsible for all the things that have happened," she admitted.

The sheriff shook his head. "Well, your theory seems sound enough, Miss Drew, but until you can offer some proof, I'm afraid I can't change my mind about the boy. If he doesn't produce the jewelry by tomorrow morning, charges will have to be instituted."

The young sleuth longed to plead further, but without proof she knew that she couldn't convince the sheriff of Ngyun's innocence. He talked for a few minutes with Ward and Maria, then the Tomiches and Heather saw him out the front door.

Nancy, sure that Ngyun must be feeling miserable, excused herself and went to the kitchen to tell him what she'd learned last night and this morning. However, when she reached the kitchen, she found it empty, the sandwich and glass of milk untouched on the table. Curious, Nancy walked to the back window and looked out across the garden just in time to see Ngyun heading toward the stable.

It took her only a moment to make a decision. She scribbled a quick note on the pad Maria kept beside the telephone, then ran out into the warm, sunny afternoon. By the time she reached the stable, Ngyun was already leading Cochise out the other side. Nancy didn't try to stop him, preferring instead to follow him.

If the sheriff wanted proof, the answer had to lie with Ngyun, she reasoned. Since he didn't seem able to explain what was happening to him, it was up to her to find the clues. Following him on one of his excursions seemed the best place to start. Nancy saddled Pepper Pot once again and set off in pursuit of the rapidly disappearing pinto.

The young detective rode for nearly an hour, catching only occasional glimpses of Ngyun and his hurrying mount. The boy never seemed to look back as he guided the pinto further and further into the low hills that marked the area of the resort closest to the Superstition Mountains.

They were practically in the shadows of the mountains when the boy finally stopped and slipped off Cochise. Leaving the pinto to graze in a small hollow, his trailing reins "ground-hitching" him so he wouldn't run away, Ngyun began to climb up a nearby, rocky outcropping.

Nancy stopped Pepper Pot at the edge of the same small patch of grass, trying to decide what to do. She meant to talk to the boy, but she didn't want him to think she was chasing him. With that in mind, she dismounted and let Pepper Pot join the pinto while she strolled across the grass and halted at the base of the rocky rise.

Ngyun turned to look at her when the horses snorted their greetings to each other, and Nancy could see the quick flash of fear in his dark, almond eyes. Then, to her surprise, he lifted a finger to his lips, cautioning her not to make any noise. When she nodded her understanding, he signalled her to climb up beside him. Curious, Nancy made her way up the steep incline, being careful not to create a landslide.

As they neared the top of the rugged hill, Ngyun again signalled caution, but this time Nancy had already heard the sounds coming from below. There were people somewhere beyond the rim above them, and it sounded very much as though they were pounding or digging!

15

Caught!

For a moment, Nancy stood stock-still. Then she moved the last few feet and peered over the rim.

In this spot, the cliffs of the Superstitions had formed the walls of what appeared to be a small canyon, well concealed by brush and rocky outcroppings.

Two men, one tall and blond, the other short, wiry, and dark, appeared to be digging in the cliff at the end of the canyon! A small, rough cabin had been erected in the center clear area, and there was a corral next to it.

What brought a gasp from Nancy, however, was one of the horses that stood in the corral. It was a pinto and looked almost exactly like Cochise!

Nancy looked at Ngyun, who had silently crept

up next to her. Together, they watched the men for several minutes, then Nancy let herself slip and slide back down the rocky rise to the grass. The boy followed at once.

"Who are those men, Ngyun?" she asked, keeping her voice low so the sound wouldn't carry.

Ngyun shrugged. "Prospectors, I think."

"On the resort land?" Nancy frowned. "Chuck and Heather never mentioned it."

"This belong to resort?" Ngyun seemed surprised.

Nancy looked around, trying to recognize the landmarks that Chuck and Heather had pointed out to her during their first days with the McGuires. Finally, she was sure. "The boundary of their land is supposed to be along that purple cliff there," she said, pointing off to the right. "The men must be on the resort land."

"Maybe they find gold," Ngyun suggested with a timid smile that was quickly gone. "Make everybody happy."

"Have you seen those men around here before?" Nancy asked.

The boy moved nervously, not meeting her gaze. "I watch here sometimes."

"Have they seen you?" Nancy asked, sensing that

there was more to the story, something that he wasn't telling her.

For a moment, he didn't answer. Then he sighed. "One time. Not here. They out in wash that go from canyon. I ride up. See what they do. They get angry. Big one shoot at me. I not come this way a while."

"They shot at you?" Nancy gasped, unable to believe her ears.

Ngyun nodded. "I not do anything. I just ride up to look, honest."

"I believe you," Nancy assured him. "Do you think they were prospecting for gold in that wash?"

Ngyun nodded. "They do same thing prospectors do in mountains. I watch a lot. I see plenty."

Nancy considered his words for a moment, then changed the subject. "Where were you going today?" she asked. "Why did you leave the resort without telling anyone?"

The thin face closed and the boy's eyes skittered away from hers once again. "I go for ride."

Nancy said nothing, sure that the boy would tell her more if she waited. He quickly proved her correct.

"I run away," Ngyun admitted at last. "I no go back."

"But you can't do that," Nancy protested. "Your aunt and uncle love you, they'd never let you leave them."

"They send me away. They think I steal. The sheriff tell them I bad. I not take jewelry, so I no can give back. They take Cochise away." Tears filled the sad, dark eyes. "He mine, I not steal him."

Understanding the boy's feelings, but sure that she couldn't let him go, Nancy took a deep breath and began to tell him what had happened to her the night before. She described how she'd followed the pinto horse into the wash and nearly died for it.

As she talked, Ngyun nodded. "Horse like one in canyon," he said when she finished. "Maybe he ride that horse?"

Nancy smiled at him. "That's what I think," she confirmed.

"What you do?" Ngyun asked. "How you find out?"

"Do they ever leave the canyon?" Nancy inquired instead of answering.

Ngyun thought for a moment, then nodded. "Sometimes. Why?"

"I want to search that cabin," Nancy answered. "If they are the ones causing all the trouble that has happened to you, there should be some clues down

there. Something that will tell me why they are trying to frame you."

Ngyun grinned at her. "I make them chase me,"
he told her. "You go down cliff."

Nancy shook her head. "That's too dangerous. If
they shot at you before, they might . . ." She was
given no chance to finish, as the boy raced across to
Cochise and jumped into the saddle. Ngyun waved
to her, smiling as he rode away.

The young detective hesitated, afraid for the boy,
yet longing for the chance to prove him innocent of
the charges that the sheriff would be bringing
against him. Finally, she sighed and made her way
to the top of the rocky cliff. She stretched out on her
stomach again so she could look down into the huge
ravine.

It seemed only a few moments before Ngyun appeared in the mouth of the canyon. When no one
noticed him, he began to shout at the two men. His
words were jumbled, but she could make out
"thief" and "gold."

The men hesitated only a few seconds before they
dropped their picks and shovels and raced to the
corral to get their horses. In no time, they had saddled up and ridden out of the corral.

Once they disappeared around the rocks at the

mouth of the canyon in pursuit of Ngyun, Nancy cautiously edged over the lip of the outcropping. Her toes sought and found a narrow ledge, and in a second she was climbing down toward the canyon floor.

Since she slipped and slid a good part of the way, the climb took only a few minutes. Once she reached the base of the wall, she could see that the men had, indeed, been digging into the rocky soil of the cliffs. Still, she didn't take time to study their prospecting, preferring to head immediately for the small cabin.

Once safely inside the squeaky door, she paused to look around and catch her breath. There was little to see. A table and two stools stood by the single window, and two unmade cots were pushed against the other walls. A single, rough shelf held meager supplies and utensils for cooking and eating. There was no sign of a stove, and provisions consisted mostly of canned goods and crackers.

Since there was not much to search, Nancy went immediately to the old, brass-bound trunk that stood beside the door. It creaked slightly as she opened it. Then she gasped. Beautiful pieces of jewelry were scattered on top of a jumble of clothing!

Silver and turquoise were spread out in lavish array. Semiprecious stones set in imaginatively worked, silver settings made two squash-blossom necklaces outstanding. The same delicate workmanship and design were repeated in a bracelet and in the setting around the single, large turquoise of a ring. Nancy nodded to herself, confident that she had found the Bascombs' stolen property.

Carefully, she shifted the jewelry to look under it, hoping for some clue to the identity of the thieves. However, when the faded denims and torn, red flannel shirt were moved, she found only a battered old book. "Big Jake Harris's journal," she murmured. "So they took that, too, and probably set the cottage on fire to get it."

Nancy sat back on her heels, frowning at the contents of the trunk. Should she leave everything here and go for the sheriff? Or should she take the shirt, the journal, and the jewelry with her? It was a hard decision.

It would be best if the sheriff saw the stolen items himself, she knew. But she was also afraid that Ngyun's appearance might have been enough to frighten the men into leaving with the treasure. She suspected that they would come back and take the things away while she was riding to the resort for help.

Suddenly, she heard sounds from outside—hoof-beats coming closer and closer!

Nancy scrambled to her feet and moved to the window, peering through the dirty glass. To her horror, she recognized the riders as the returning prospectors. They were already so close she could hear their voices clearly.

"Did you see where he went, Sam?" the blond man asked his smaller companion.

"Little brat ducked into those rocks and just disappeared," the darker man replied, riding into the corral. "What do you think we should do, Joe?"

The big man shrugged as he dismounted. "Maybe nobody will believe him," he suggested hopefully. "I heard that the sheriff was at the resort today, so the kid is in a lot of trouble over the jewelry we stole."

The men chuckled evilly as they closed the corral gate and stood in the shade of the cabin wall. "Mr. Henry isn't going to like it, if the kid talks to anybody about us," Sam observed.

Nancy gasped. Was the McGuires' friendly neighbor her unknown enemy?

"So what do you want me to do?" Joe demanded. "Do you want to ride to the ranch and tell him the kid was out here again?"

Sam shook his head. "He's coming out tonight, anyway. Said he wanted to look over what we've

142

dug out so far. He doesn't think we're in the right place yet."

"He'll change his mind when he sees the nugget you found this afternoon," Joe said. "This has to be where the gold washed out of the mountains in the flood last spring, 'cause this is the end of the ravine. We've prospected every other inch of it on his ranch and on this one."

"Don't tell me," the little man said. "Let's just see what else we can uncover before dark."

"Whatever you say, Sam," Joe replied with a sigh, "but I'm getting mighty hungry."

The men moved away from the cabin, still talking in low voices, but Nancy could no longer make out the words. She watched them till they reached the cliff face and took up their picks and shovels, then she leaned against the wall and looked around.

There was no way out. The door and window were both on the side of the cabin, facing the spot where the men were working. Nancy nibbled at her lip. The land all the way around was totally open, so the men couldn't miss seeing her the moment she stepped through the rough, squeaky door. She was trapped, and it was only a matter of time before someone came inside and found her!

16

A Great Shock

Nancy looked around the small room once again, then crossed to the trunk and carefully returned it to its original condition. That done, she assessed the situation, seeking some solution. But none came.

The only hiding place appeared to be beneath one of the cots. The area was tiny, but the blankets, carelessly thrown off, hung to the floor and would give her some protection.

Having decided where she could hide, Nancy returned to the window to watch the men as they dug lazily in the crumbling cliff face. Gold! That had to be the answer.

The mention of Mr. Henry had been a terrible shock. He'd been so friendly to the McGuires, so helpful, according to Heather and Chuck. Yet she did remember that Heather had said he'd once offered to buy the ranch.

An hour dragged by, then another. The men worked without enthusiasm, taking frequent breaks in the shade of an old mesquite tree that grew beside a small spring. Nancy watched longingly as they dipped up the water. She was both hot and thirsty in the dusty cabin.

When the shadows moved across the floor of the canyon, the men stopped working, throwing down their picks and shovels and heading for the cabin. Terrified, Nancy slid into her small hiding place.

Heart pounding, she crouched in the dark space and waited as the two men argued about which cans to open for dinner and what they should tell Mr. Henry about Ngyun. Sam wanted to keep it a secret, while Joe muttered dark predictions of what their boss would do to them if he found out that they hadn't told him. She was glad when they went back outside to put the grill over their small campfire.

The smell of the heating food soon penetrated the cabin, and Nancy became aware of her own hunger. She couldn't stay hidden here forever, she realized. But what to do? She couldn't slip away, even after dark, for the men were cooking only a few feet from the door.

Uncomfortable in the stuffy darkness under the cot, Nancy shifted her weight and tried to stretch her cramped legs. But her riding boot caught in the blanket, which in turn caught around the leg of the unsteady cot. To her horror, the whole frame shifted, tipped a little, then rocked back against the wall with a loud bang.

At once, there were shouts from outside, and the next minute the men burst into the cabin.

Nancy did not dare breathe, but with one man holding the lantern and the other searching the room, they discovered her almost immediately.

"Look what we've got here!" Sam shouted as he pulled the girl from underneath the cot. "A spy!"

"Just what we need," Joe grumbled. "I wonder what—"

He was interrupted by another man who at that moment walked through the door. *Mr. Henry!*

"Well, if it isn't the nosy Miss Nancy Drew," the rancher said. "You certainly are a stubborn young woman. Anyone with normal good sense would have paid attention to the letter I sent." He smiled evilly. "Or to the scorpion I put in your suitcase."

"You know her, boss?" Sam asked, his dark eyes bright with curiosity.

"She's the one you shot the arrow at, you idiot,"

Mr. Henry snapped. "If your aim had been better, we wouldn't be having this problem."

"Ain't my fault she moved after I let go of the arrow!" Sam grumbled.

"How did you get out of the wash before the flood, Miss Drew?" Mr. Henry asked, ignoring his employee. "Sam said he had a tough time escaping the water with you so close behind him."

"I got out," Nancy said curtly. "And I didn't get hurt in the station wagon, either, when you forced us off the road the day we arrived."

Mr. Henry did not deny that he had caused the accident; he just glared at her. "Too bad!" he sneered.

"What do you want to do with her, boss?" Joe asked.

Mr. Henry sighed. "I suppose we might as well tie her up till I can think of a convincing accident for her. We certainly can't let her leave here since she obviously knows what is going on."

"What is going on, Mr. Henry?" Nancy asked, hoping to sound innocent.

"Get some rope, Joe," Mr. Henry ordered, then gripped Nancy's arm tightly.

Nancy drew in a deep breath, waiting till Joe was in the cabin and Sam had his back to her. It was a desperate move, she realized, but her choices were very limited. She lifted one foot and brought the heel of her boot down on Mr. Henry's instep with all her strength. He bellowed in pain and rage, but most important, he let go of her arm!

Nancy plunged wildly out of the flickering light of the campfire and into the deep shadows of the brush and trees that grew near the small spring. Once in their concealment, she paused, not sure what to do next. She'd escaped for the moment, but she had a terrible feeling that she was only delaying whatever Mr. Henry had planned. There was nowhere to run!

"Block the canyon entrance!" Mr. Henry was shouting. "Put more wood on the fire. Get torches. We can't let her escape us now!"

Nancy moved cautiously in the brush, grateful that the rain had kept it from becoming dry. Any loud crackling of twigs or branches would give her location away. As her eyes adjusted to the darkness, she saw the rocky hillside ahead and moved toward it, seeking a large rock or depression where she could hide while she tried to decide on her next move.

There was little choice, but the biggest of the rocky formations did offer a small, cup-shaped hole behind it. Nancy slipped into the hole and snuggled down against the still-warm earth as the cold of the desert night began to seep through her light shirt.

The crashing and shouting from the cabin area continued for quite some time as the men began to spread out to search. Then, suddenly, everything grew very, very quiet. Nancy, who'd been crouching low in fear, lifted her head, sensing at once that something had happened.

She heard the tattoo of approaching hoofbeats, and suddenly the air was full of shouts and shots. Nancy got to her feet, recognizing the voices that were calling her name.

"George, Bess, Heather, Chuck!" She ran through the brush and into the arms of her friends.

For several minutes, they all talked at once. Then, as the first relief died away, Nancy looked around. She saw that Ward, Chuck, and the sheriff were holding rifles on Mr. Henry and his two men.

"How . . . how did you get here?" Nancy asked.

"Ngyun came riding into the resort about an hour ago, shouting that you were in terrible danger," Heather replied. "We didn't know what to think, but he insisted that we call the sheriff. When he calmed down a little, he described Leaning Tree Ravine and Canyon to us, so we knew where to find you."

"Thank goodness he did," Nancy breathed, feeling a little weak with relief now that the danger was over.

The sheriff walked up and addressed Nancy. "Are you going to tell us what is going on here, Miss Drew? Mr. Henry is claiming that you sent for him. He says you had some complaint that his men were trespassing on the McGuire Ranch."

"This is McGuire land, isn't it?" Nancy asked, shocked by the man's quick lies.

Everyone nodded.

"Well," Nancy began, "his men have been doing more here than just trespassing."

It took nearly an hour of answering questions for the sheriff, helping him to search the cabin so he could examine the contents of the old trunk, and interrogating Mr. Henry before everything was completely explained. The rancher admitted to setting the fires and being responsible for the other incidents that were blamed on Ngyun. The boy was innocent of all the crimes of which he'd been accused.

Finally, Nancy asked, "Is it possible that there really is a valuable gold mine in this canyon, sheriff?"

"Probably not a mine," the sheriff replied. "You see, when we have bad floods like we did last spring, shelves of rock and shale break loose from

151

the sides of the ravines or from cliffs like those over there." He indicated the end of the canyon where the men had been digging. "When that happens, small pockets or short veins of gold are sometimes uncovered. I suspect that's what has happened here."

"You mean we have gold on our land?" Heather asked.

"What do you say to that, Henry?" the sheriff asked.

Mr. Henry glared at them all, then shrugged. "We haven't found too much yet, but it has to be here in the canyon. I discovered a couple of nuggets late last fall when we were cleaning the debris out of our end of Leaning Tree Ravine. I figured it was coming from somewhere along the ravine itself, so I made you the offer on your land in case I didn't find it on my property."

· "You would have bought the resort for the gold?" Heather sounded skeptical.

He shook his head. "If you'd taken my offer, the gold would have been pure profit. The land is worth that much, anyway."

"But we didn't take it," Chuck reminded him.

"And we didn't find any gold on our end of the ravine. We went over every inch. These two idiots were supposed to casually check your territory, but they let that sneaky kid catch them digging around in the ravine not far from here."

"So what?" Nancy asked.

"So they couldn't risk having him talk about what he'd seen." Mr. Henry's face was cold.

"So that's when you decided to see to it that Ngyun was sent away?" Ward looked as though he'd like to hit the handcuffed man.

"He never said a word to us about seeing the men," Heather murmured. "I wonder why."

"He just thought they were prospectors," Nancy answered. "He didn't even know this was your land. He's seen lots of people prospecting in the mountains."

"Well, we all know whose land it is, and now we know what has been going on," the sheriff said. "I suggest that we get our horses and head for the resort. It's a long ride over rough country and it's getting late. Where is your horse, Miss Drew?"

"Up there," Nancy said, pointing to the side of the canyon. "At least, I hope he still is."

"If you left the reins trailing, Pepper Pot is still there," Heather assured her. "He's very well trained."

"I'll take you up there, Nancy," George offered. "You can ride double with me. Let's go get him while they finish up everything down here."

Nancy nodded, suddenly glad to be getting away from the canyon and all the frightening things that had happened to her here. She was proud of having solved one of her mysteries and having cleared Ngyun's name, but her mind was already returning to the second mystery—that of the Kachina spirits that still haunted the resort!

17

Celebration

Once they reached the resort and the sheriff left with his prisoners, Maria served a huge meal, restoring Nancy's good spirits. She and Ngyun told and retold their stories of what had happened during the long afternoon and evening.

Nancy was just finishing a detailed description of how she'd managed to escape her captors when Heather spoke up, changing the subject. "I know this is a nice dinner and everything, but I think we should have a real celebration," she began.

"What do you mean?" Nancy asked.

"How about a party for all our friends and neighbors? I'm sure they'd love to meet Nancy and hear about what she has done. And it will give everyone a chance to make Ngyun feel welcome in the area after all the trouble he's had." She paused, then asked, "What do you think?"

"How about having it tomorrow night?" Chuck suggested. "It could be a welcome home for Grandfather, too."

"Is he coming back?" Heather asked. "Why didn't you tell me?"

"Actually, I've been too busy. In case you've forgotten, I was talking on the phone to him when Ngyun rode in, and after that . . ." He broke off with a grin.

"What kind of a party shall we have?" Maria asked.

"How about a barn dance?" Heather suggested.

"Don't you need a barn for that?" Bess asked. "I mean, your stable is very nice, but there isn't any room for dancing." She looked around. "That is what you do at a barn dance, isn't it?"

Heather laughed. "As a matter of fact, we do have a barn, a genuine, old relic from the days shortly after Jake Harris died."

"You do?" Nancy frowned. "I don't remember seeing it."

"You haven't," Chuck confirmed. "Or rather, you saw it, but you didn't know what it was."

"What are you two talking about?" George asked.

"How could we see it and not know what it was? A barn is a barn."

"True," Chuck conceded. "What I meant was— we drove by the barn on our way here, but you didn't know it was our barn. You see, after Jake's death, there were all kinds of rumors about this old house. People were always claiming to see lights in it at night, things like that. Anyway, the people who took over the ranch didn't want to live here, so they built a small house and a barn on what was then the trail to town. We passed it on our way here from the airport."

"And the house?" George said. "I don't remember seeing any house that close."

"The house burned down years ago," Heather answered. "We talked about tearing the barn down, but then we decided that our guests might enjoy an old-fashioned barn dance from time to time, so we fixed it up instead. Now what do you think of the idea, Nancy?"

"I think it sounds just fantastic," Nancy told her. "I can hardly wait."

Heather got up from the table. "You folks enjoy dessert," she said. "I'm going to start making some phone calls. We'll never be ready if I don't."

"And I'd better start planning the menu," Maria

decided. "We'll need lots of food and some punch, of course."

"What can we do?" Bess asked. "Can't we help?"

"You can be the cleaning and decorating committee," Chuck told them. "That way, Heather will be free to help Maria with the cooking." He paused, then added, "The barn is weather-tight, so it isn't real dirty, but it will need sweeping out and some kind of decorations."

"We'll do it," George agreed, "if we can borrow the jeep tomorrow. We'll have to go into town to get the decorations."

"It's yours," Chuck told them. "In fact, you could use the station wagon in the morning, if you like. I will have to have it in the afternoon, though, to pick up Grandfather."

"The jeep will be fine for us," Nancy told him, her eyes sparkling at the prospect of a party. "Besides, it may take us till afternoon to decide what we're going to use for decorations. We haven't even seen this barn yet, you know."

The rest of the evening passed quickly as plans for the party grew. Still, Nancy managed to slip away for a little while to follow Ngyun to the stable, where she found him leaning on the stall door, petting Cochise.

"He mine forever now," he said, looking up at her. "I thank you."

"And I thank you," Nancy replied. "If you hadn't come back here and sent help, I could never have escaped. You were very brave."

"I try keep men away," he went on. "They almost catch me. I hide. I sorry they go back."

"You did just fine," Nancy reassured him. "We're a great team."

Smiling at each other and laughing together, they gave Cochise and Pepper Pot each a final pat, then went back to the house.

Everyone was still working on plans for the party, which was to include a number of the children in the area and their parents, as well as young people of Chuck and Heather's age. By the time she said good night, Nancy had decided that it had been a truly satisfactory evening after all the bad hours she'd spent in the canyon.

The next day dawned clear and beautiful, but Nancy woke with a feeling that all was not well. As soon as she opened her bedroom door, her premonition was confirmed. George was standing in the hall looking very unhappy. Nancy quickly asked her what was wrong.

"It's back," George announced.

"What is back?" Nancy asked.

"The Kachina ghost. Bess and I saw it last night."

"You what?" Nancy frowned. "Where did you see it? Was it in the hall?"

George shook her head. "Outside. I thought I heard something, and when I went to the window, it was over on that little ridge. I thought maybe I was seeing things, but Bess woke up and she saw it, too."

"What was it doing?"

"Just watching the resort. At least, it didn't do anything else while we were looking at it."

Nancy sighed. "I wish I'd seen it."

"What would you have done?" George asked.

"I don't know," Nancy admitted. "Maybe asked it for a clue." She forced a laugh.

"It probably would have given you one, too," George told her, joining in her laughter.

"Well, I guess we'll have to wait to find out," Nancy said. "Now, how about some breakfast? I think we're going to have a very busy day, don't you?"

"The way Heather has been planning, I'd say so."

The barn proved to be a real challenge—one that they met with brooms, mops, and dust cloths. Once it was clean, there were decorations to be decided on. A trip into Apache Junction provided a wide selection of colorful Mexican hats and baskets, which they stuffed with bright paper flowers.

Ward and Chuck brought in a half-dozen bales of hay for makeshift benches, and a number of folding tables and chairs for the more conventional guests. Paper streamers and more flowers were draped from the rafters to finish the effect, and the barn was quite festive by the time Nancy and her friends were through. They were feeling quite pleased with themselves as they drove back to the resort to have dinner and change for the party, which was scheduled to begin at seven sharp.

Dinner was a very simple meal, and they ate by the pool so they wouldn't get in Maria's way as she finished fixing the food for Ward and Chuck to take to the barn. Mr. McGuire, a friendly, white-haired man with a white mustache, was now happily settled in a lounge chair, his wrist still in a cast and his knee resting comfortably on a padded cushion.

As soon as Nancy filled her plate, he signaled her to his side. "I want to hear all about your finding Big Jake's journal," he said. "Chuck barely mentioned it on the way home. He was too busy telling me about your adventures in the canyon at the end of Leaning Tree Ravine."

"That's a strange name for that ravine," Nancy observed. "I don't remember seeing a single tree, let alone one that was leaning."

"It was named for an old palo verde tree that died years ago, I think." Mr. McGuire laughed. "The story was that when the tree was blown over, the roots were full of gold."

"Gold?" Nancy raised an eyebrow.

He shook his head. "I don't believe it either. Most of the washes and ravines have names like that and stories to go with them. We may change that one to Golden Gulch, however, if there is a pocket of gold in the cliffs of the canyon."

"That would be quite appropriate," Nancy told him. "I hope it works out."

"Now, what about the Kachina you saw? Tell me all about it. What was it like?"

"Well, to begin with, it was the Cloud Kachina, or at least it looked like the Cloud Kachina painting." Nancy did her best to tell him everything that she'd seen and heard that night.

Once she'd completed her story, Mr. McGuire began describing his experience with the same spirit. When he finished, he asked, "Do you think that was the solution? Finding the journal, I mean. Have you routed our resident ghost?"

Nancy sighed and put down her fork. "I'm afraid not."

"What do you mean? Have you seen the thing again?"

Nancy shook her head. "I haven't, but George and Bess saw a Kachina on the ridge outside last night, and I've heard the chanting every night I've been here." The young sleuth sighed. "I don't know what it means, but I'm sure there is more to this mystery, and I'm still trying to solve it."

"Well, you just watch yourself," Mr. McGuire told her. "I don't want you to end up in the hospital the way I did. You have taken altogether too many chances already."

"I'll be careful," Nancy assured him. The conversation was ended by Heather's announcement that they had less than an hour to get ready for their guests.

The moment she entered her room, Nancy sensed a change. She looked around quickly, seeking a reason for the feeling. At first, everything seemed to be in order. Then she saw that the bedspread had been disturbed.

Remembering the incident with the scorpion, Nancy approached the bed cautiously, not sure what to expect. However, when she eased the spread back, no dangerous creature awaited her. Instead, she found a feather lying in the fold of the heavy material!

It was very old and slightly dusty, and when Nancy picked it up, she gasped. She recognized it as being from the headdress of the Kachina spirit she had followed in the hall!

18

Barn Dance

Nancy stood quite still, her heart pounding. Then she heard the soft sounds of chanting once again. She ran quickly to the window, then to the hall, but there was no sign of the Kachina spirit in either place.

Disappointed, Nancy sat down on the bed. She realized the feather was a message or perhaps a summons, but she had no idea what it meant!

Swallowing a sigh, she placed the feather carefully in the drawer of her bedside table and turned her attention to what she had come to her room to do. She had to get dressed—the celebration was about to begin!

Nancy donned the blue-and-white gingham peasant dress that she'd bought while they were in

Apache Junction shopping for decorations, and studied her reflection in the mirror. The square neckline with its feminine, white ruffles was very becoming, and the blue ribbon sash made her waist look tiny above the full, swinging skirt. White sandals and a white crocheted shawl completed the outfit, and she felt very festive.

Nancy had already decided not to mention the feather when she stepped out of her room. She smiled easily at Bess and George, who were waiting in the hall. Both girls were clad in dresses similar in style to Nancy's—George's in shades of gold and brown, Bess's in a rose that brought out the pink in her cheeks.

Bess twirled on her toes. "Don't you just *feel* like dancing in a dress like this?"

Nancy laughed. "You'd feel like dancing in jeans and cowboy boots," she teased.

"Well, of course I would," Bess admitted, "but this is better. I hope Chuck likes it."

Nancy laughed. "I know he will."

"Let's go," Heather called from the lobby. "I hope you don't mind walking. It's only a little more than half a mile, and both our vehicles are loaded with food."

"Lead the way," Nancy told her.

The path they followed was clear of rocks and led

up to a ridge, then wound gently down the other side to where the barn sat near the road. As they descended the hill, Nancy could see the jeep and the station wagon at the rear door of the barn, while several other cars were already parked in front of the well-lit, old building.

Lanterns glowed in all the windows and light spilled out the open doors. As the girls drew closer, they could hear the sounds of the band tuning up their fiddles and guitars.

Floyd, Tim, Diana, and the rest of their companions from the night of the barbecue were waiting near their cars. As soon as they had greeted the girls, they all went inside. Once they began dancing, they were joined by dozens of other couples.

It was a fine party, but different from any Nancy had ever attended. Whole families arrived, some bringing food which was delivered to what had once been the feed or tack room of the barn.

Babies were settled in baskets on the hay bales, while children Ngyun's age and younger ran in and out, laughing and playing. Everyone seemed to know and like everyone else, and they all greeted Mr. McGuire warmly and congratulated Nancy on solving the mystery that had surrounded Ngyun and the theft of the turquoise jewelry.

The music the band played was a mixture of coun-

167

try-western tunes, square dances, modern pop, and old favorites—something to please everyone. Nancy found herself with a different partner for every dance and had to plead exhaustion before she was allowed to stop.

Floyd escorted her to the punch bowl which rested on a table opposite the small bandstand, and poured a glass for each of them.

"How do you like our country dance, Nancy?" he asked.

"I love it," Nancy admitted enthusiastically, "but I don't know where some of the people get all their energy. That older couple out there hasn't missed a single dance—fast or slow."

Floyd laughed. "They're my grandparents, and you can bet they'll stay on the floor all night. They are members of a championship square dance club, so they're in terrific shape."

Bess and Chuck came over to join them. Bess accepted a glass of punch, then asked, "When do they serve all the goodies I saw Maria fixing?"

Chuck laughed. "Bess, your appetite is incredible!" Then he looked at his watch. "In about half an hour," he said. "We try to serve the food early enough so the children can eat before they wander out to the cars to sleep."

"Is that what happens?" Nancy asked. "I wondered, with so many children here."

"Everyone brings blankets, and when the younger ones get sleepy, their parents just settle them in their cars."

"Sounds simple enough," Bess observed.

Chuck nodded. "Well, a couple of times people have gotten home and discovered they have the wrong child, but since everyone knows everybody else, they just settle it with a phone call and trade back in the morning."

Nancy and Bess giggled, then Floyd took Nancy's empty punch glass and set it on the table before whirling her back out onto the dance floor. The time passed pleasantly, and when the feast was spread out, they were ready to do it justice. The hard exercise on the dance floor had whetted every appetite.

Later, however, when the music grew slower and the crowd had thinned a little, Nancy slipped outside alone for a breath of air. The night was clear, and though the moon was no longer full, it was still quite large enough to give plenty of light to the now familiar desert landscape.

She moved away from the barn into the quiet of the desert, hearing the distant howling of coyotes as they serenaded the moon in their own fashion. Just then, a movement on the ridge that hid the resort from her view caught her eye.

Nancy's heart pounded as she recognized her guide from the previous night, the Cloud Kachina! It moved with ghostly grace along the rough ground. The moonlight glinted on the white feathers that adorned its colorful face mask, giving it almost a halo effect.

Nancy gasped as it seemed to turn her way and gesture with one red, yellow, and white–painted arm. It wanted her to follow it!

Everything else forgotten, and totally without fear, Nancy turned her steps in that direction, cutting across the rougher ground to save time as she hurried after the apparition. As she neared the top of the ridge, the spirit vanished from her view, and for a moment she was afraid that she had misunderstood the signal and perhaps frightened it. However, when she reached the crest, she could see it ahead of her, drifting unhurriedly toward the resort.

Breathless with excitement, the young detective followed the ghostly spirit as it skirted the old, stone structure. It led her around the front, into the shadows on the side of the building opposite from where her room was located.

Few lights were burning in the windows on this

end of the building. However, the moonlight on the white feathers made the Kachina visible even as it ventured into the brush and trees that grew in thorny profusion near the wall.

Nancy stopped, unsure what to do. The Kachina halted, too, barely noticeable behind the mesquite and cactus that protected the wall of the building. Once again, the arm signaled for her to approach. Nancy obeyed slowly, feeling in her dress pocket for the matches she'd put there when she'd helped Maria light the candles on the serving table.

"Too bad you spirits don't supply flashlights," she told the apparition as she approached, making her way cautiously, not wanting to snag her new dress on any of the thorny plants.

The Kachina remained in place till Nancy was almost close enough to touch it. Suddenly, it was gone! Nancy hesitated, then carefully lit a match. The light helped only a little, but she did catch a glimpse of color low on the wall before the match sputtered out.

The next one lasted longer as she held it down near the ground so she could see what was painted on the wall. A fierce-looking Kachina stared back at her from the slits of its black mask, and Nancy shivered though the night was mild.

Several more matches showed no further clues.

There was only a single painting and it was too dark for her to study it. She finally left the shadows of the house.

She'd wanted a clue, and now the Kachina spirit had given her one! The only trouble was, she had no idea what it might mean. With a sigh, she started back toward the barn, aware that her friends might have missed her and that they would worry if they had.

Floyd was waiting for her when she reached the foot of the hill. "I've been watching for you," he told her. "Where were you?"

"Out to get some air," Nancy said, deciding not to mention the ghost just yet. "Did I miss anything?"

"Not much. The band took a break and Mr. McGuire gave a little speech, explaining to everyone what happened. He praised you for your excellent sleuthing, and Ngyun for his bravery. The boy really loved it; he's quite the star of the evening."

Nancy laughed. "He deserves it after all he's been through."

"Well, he does share the limelight with you, Nancy!"

Nancy blushed. "My job isn't done yet," she said. "I haven't solved the Kachina's secret yet!"

"You will," Floyd said with a chuckle. "And I bet it won't take long, either."

"I'm certainly going to try," Nancy replied, thinking of the painting her elusive guide had shown her tonight. Tomorrow, in daylight, perhaps she'd be able to make some sense out of the strange, little Kachina with its ferocious appearance!

19

A Ghost Beckons

After she got into bed that night, Nancy opened the drawer of the bedside table and took out the feather. She held it lightly, studying it, wondering what the morning would bring, then she laid it gently on the other pillow before she went to sleep.

Thanks to her impatience, she woke early in spite of the late night. When she was dressed, she armed herself with some stout clippers from the pool storage shed and made her way around to the far side of the old, stone building.

It took her several minutes to locate the small painting. Once she did, she spent nearly half an hour clearing away the worst of the growth in front of it. Even when she'd finished, she wasn't surprised that no one had found the painting before. It was in a hidden spot, shielded by the very unevenness of the wall itself. If it hadn't been for her guide, she would never have found it.

Suddenly, there was a sound behind her, and she whirled around, startled.

Ngyun had come up to her and pointed at the picture. "What that?" he asked.

"I found another Kachina painting," Nancy replied, then told the boy about her mysterious guide the night before.

"It not like others," Ngyun observed after he'd inspected the painting.

"I know," Nancy agreed. "Is your Aunt Maria awake yet?"

"She fixing breakfast."

"Would you mind asking her to come out here when she has a free minute? I'd like to know what this Kachina represents. Then maybe I can figure out why it is in such a hidden spot."

"I go ask," Ngyun agreed, and disappeared around the stone wall at a dead run.

Nancy busied herself clearing away more thorny limbs. She had a fair space opened up by the time Maria and Ngyun came to join her. She got to her feet and moved to one side so that the Indian woman could have a clear view of the small but surprisingly well-preserved picture.

Maria leaned down, then gasped and stepped back, almost involuntarily. "It's *Hilili!*" she whispered.

"*Hilili?* What's that?" Nancy asked. "Is it some special sort of Kachina?"

"It is a Witch Kachina brought to our tribe from the Zuni. You see the wildcat skin draped over its shoulders? It's a mark of fierceness. It is often a guard at our ceremonials."

"A guard?" Nancy frowned. "But why would it be painted here?"

"To guard the house?" Maria suggested.

"I don't think so. A guard would be near the door." Nancy studied the painting again, then asked, "Is it authentic? Jake didn't add or change anything, did he?"

Maria bent down and examined the picture carefully. "I've seen several, and this looks exactly like the old ones," she declared. She peered at the heavy growth of cactus and thorny bushes on each side. "How in the world did you find it?"

"The Cloud Kachina brought me here last night," Nancy answered. "It was trying to tell me something, and—" she added with a sparkle in her eyes, "I think I know what it was!"

Maria stared at her, realizing what Nancy meant. But her dark face showed no emotion. Instead, she firmly took Nancy's hand. "Before you go any further, I think you should come in and have some sausage and pancakes."

Nancy giggled. "I might as well."

"What you think?" Ngyun inquired curiously, tugging at her hand.

"You'll find out in a little while," Nancy told him.

When they joined Bess, George, Heather, and Chuck around the kitchen table, the others sensed immediately that Nancy was up to something.

"Are you going to tell us what is on your mind?" George asked. "You've been sitting there looking like a cat with canary feathers on her whiskers."

"Have you made a discovery?" Bess added curiously.

"As a matter of fact, I think I have." Nancy smiled at them. "As soon as you're all through with breakfast, I have something to show you."

With such a promise, plates were quickly emptied, and everyone followed Nancy out into the sun and around to the side of the house. She pointed out the small painting and explained how she'd been guided to it by the ghostly Kachina.

"I don't understand how you can follow those things," Heather said with a shiver. "I'd be scared to death to even see one up close."

"But it has been helping us!" Nancy reminded

her. "First, it showed me where to look for the journal, now this."

"What does it mean?" Chuck asked. "Have you figured that out?"

"Well, Maria gave me the best clue," Nancy answered. "She says this is *Hilili,* a guard Kachina."

"So?" George asked, when Nancy paused.

"So I think it was painted here because it's guarding something," Nancy replied.

"The treasure?" Bess gasped.

"Nancy, really?" Heather asked.

Nancy shrugged. "We won't know till we do some digging," she told them.

"I'll get the shovels," Chuck said. "You decide where to dig."

Nancy studied the area, trying to judge the age of the various plants. Then she noticed that Hilili was holding a single thin, green, yucca leaf whip in one hand and that it seemed to be set at an odd angle, unlike the several whips in its other hand. With her eyes, she traced the direction in which the painted leaf was pointing and marked the sandy soil with her toe.

"Is that where the treasure is buried?" Heather asked.

"I'm afraid we'll have to dig to find out," Nancy admitted.

"So let's get started," Chuck said, handing a shovel to Nancy. "You can take out the first shovelful."

"We're going to have to take turns," Nancy warned as she started digging. "It's hard to tell how deep we have to go. She hesitated, then added, "Provided there is something buried here. I can't guarantee that, you know."

"So dig," he teased. "We'll never find anything speculating."

Soon, the laughter died away and was replaced by serious work. The hole was growing, but the earth was so hard they had to fight for every foot. Chuck and Nancy had soon given their shovels to Bess and Heather, and they in turn yielded to George and Ngyun. Maria was kept busy bringing out cold drinks and other refreshments to keep the workers going.

As it neared noon, Nancy and Chuck once more took up the shovels and stepped down into the hole. Nancy worked on one end, her hands sore and perspiration forming on her face as the day grew warmer. However, as she forced the shovel in for the fourth time, there was a dull, clanging sound, and the shovel refused to move when she leaned her weight on it.

"Hey," Chuck shouted, "you've hit something!"

"I hope it isn't another rock," Nancy said.

"That didn't sound like a rock," Chuck told her. "Let me see if I can uncover it."

Excitement made the soil fly, and in a moment the top of an old, metal trunk was uncovered. Everyone was anxious to help, and in a short time, Chuck was able to free the small trunk from the clinging earth and lift it out of the hole.

For a moment, they just stared at it. Then Mr. McGuire, who'd been watching the entire proceedings from a lawn chair in the shade, called, "Break the lock on it, Chuck. Let's open it up!"

Chuck stepped forward and used a pick to hack away the old lock, but instead of opening the trunk himself, he turned to Nancy. "I think you should do it," he said. "You're the one who found it."

Everyone nodded agreement. Nancy took a deep breath and moved forward to touch the metal lid that was warming now from the sun after being so long in the cool depths of the earth. Her hand shook as she began lifting the rusty lid!

20

Hilili's Treasure

Once the lid was open, Nancy gasped in delight as the sun touched the slightly faded, but incredibly beautiful Kachina dolls within. Maria cried out and came to kneel beside the trunk, tears running down her brown cheeks.

"What is it?" Mr. McGuire shouted, struggling to his feet and limping over to join them. "What is the treasure?"

Nancy lifted the first of the Kachinas with reverent gentleness, recognizing it at once as a replica of her guide from the night before. Time had dimmed and broken its feathers, and the paint on the color-ful mask was faded, but that only made the little carvings more precious.

"They aren't gone!" Maria whispered. "We always believed that they were taken away or destroyed when the chiefs fled to Mexico. We've mourned their loss all these years."

"There are some papers in the bottom of the trunk, Nancy," Chuck said, leaning over her shoulder. "See, under the Kachinas."

Nancy moved the dolls very carefully, slipping the dusty pages out. "From the journal," she said. "I recognize Jake Harris's handwriting, and remember, I told you some of the pages had been torn out."

"What does it say?" George asked. "What are the Kachinas doing here? Did he really take them from the Indians after all?"

"I think we should go inside with all this," Mr. McGuire said. "Nancy can read to us from the journal while the rest of us study the Kachinas."

After they were all settled in the living room, Nancy scanned the pages quickly, then began to read:

> *Deer Slayer and the other chiefs have come again and this time they left their Kachinas behind for me to guard. They say that Winslow has hired some bad men*

183

*to follow the members of the tribe and
they fear those men will steal the sacred
dolls for his collection.*

*There have been fires in the hills again.
I thought it might be Deer Slayer's people
camping nearby to protect my house, but
last night a fearsome torch was burning on
the ridge and the riders who set it were
white men. The door was not fastened
when I came home tonight, so I fear Winslow's men have been here searching for
the Kachina dolls.*

"Big Jake escaped their first visit," Bess murmured softly, "but obviously not their second one."

Nancy nodded, shifting to another page. "The
next couple of entries are about his being afraid to
go out and not knowing where to turn for help,"
Nancy told them, then went on reading.

*I fear the Kachinas will be stolen from
me if I don't hide them. I've chosen a safe
place to bury them and painted a guardian
Witch Kachina to mark the spot for Deer
Slayer if I'm not here to tell him myself.*

*Dawn is near and the fearsome torch
just beyond the door is burning out. To-*

morrow night they may burn even this house to the ground. I shall wait till daylight when they hide from my sight and I'll bury these few pages with the sacred dolls. When they come tonight, I'll have my rifle ready.

Nancy put down the stained pages. "That's all there is," she said. "He must have done what he said, buried the trunk, then barricaded himself in the house to wait."

Maria shook her head, turning her attention at last from the Kachinas, which she'd been examining very carefully. "Poor old man, he was so brave. The collector Winslow and his people must have come just as he expected, and he was so old and frail the strain killed him."

Mr. McGuire nodded. "You can bet that they were the ones that ransacked the house. And they were the ghosts that haunted it the next few years. They knew that he had the Kachinas and they were determined to find them."

"But they didn't," Heather reminded everyone with a grin. "That took someone as smart as Nancy."

"With a lot of help from the Kachinas," Nancy reminded them modestly, as she picked up the Cloud Kachina doll that had been her guide.

"So what happens to the treasure now, Mr. McGuire?" George asked. "I mean, it really is a treasure, isn't it?"

"For my people, the Kachina dolls are beyond price," Maria whispered.

"Indeed, they are extremely precious," McGuire agreed, "and they shall be returned to their rightful owners as soon as possible."

Maria turned to him, her dark eyes luminous. "You mean it?" she asked. "You know how valuable they are and they were found on your property. There are collectors who would pay any price you ask for them."

The old man smiled at her. "Your people trusted Big Jake to protect their most sacred treasure, and he managed to do so at the cost of his life. That doesn't give us any claim to them. Besides, wasn't your great-grandfather one of the chiefs who entrusted them to Jake?"

Maria nodded. "He died in exile in Mexico, driven there by those who claimed that he and the other chiefs had caused the death of Jake Harris."

"That terrible collector Winslow probably made up the story to cover his own guilt," Bess said.

Everyone nodded.

"What do you plan on doing with the Kachinas, Maria?" Nancy asked. "I mean, how will you go about returning them to your tribe?"

Maria leaned back, lost in thought for several minutes, then she smiled. "I think I would like to have Ngyun help me return them," she said. "He is a descendant of a chief, and it would truly make my brother's son a member of the tribe."

"Oh, how wonderful, Ngyun," Nancy breathed. "You'll be proud to do it, won't you?" She looked at the grinning boy.

Ngyun was too overcome to speak, but his happy face when he nodded was answer enough.

"Will you be here for the ceremonial?" Maria asked Nancy.

The girl sighed, then looked at the circle of her friends. "I'd love to," she replied, "but now that both mysteries here have been solved, I probably should be getting back to River Heights."

Little did she know that soon after her return home she would be confronted with a new mystery called *The Twin Dilemma*.

"How about lunch?" Bess suggested, changing the subject. "Finding treasures makes me hungry."

"That makes two of us." Chuck laughed and put an arm around the pretty girl. Chatting happily, the young detectives all headed for the kitchen, leaving Maria and the wide-eyed Ngyun alone with their precious Kachinas.

NANCY DREW MYSTERY STORIES®
by Carolyn Keene

You will also enjoy

THE LINDA CRAIG® SERIES
by Ann Sheldon